Sherlock Holmes
in
The Deerstalker

book by
TERENCE MUSTOO

music and lyrics by
DOUG FLACK

IAN HENRY PUBLICATIONS
1985

ISBN 0 86025 886 6

The fee for each performance of this play by amateurs in the British Isles
is Fifteen Pounds
and application for licences should be made to the publishers
IAN HENRY PUBLICATIONS, LTD.
38 Parkstone Avenue, Hornchurch, Essex, RM11 3LW

Copies of the piano score are available for hire.
Enquiries to Hornchurch (04042) 42042 or the address above.

Printed in Great Britain

CAST

Dr John H Watson
Sherlock Holmes
Mrs Hudson
Rev. Charles Samuels
Alf Barker
Lily Nightingale
Beth
Tilly
Rose
Pearl
Ruby
The Great Marvo
Bob
Tom
Jim
Old Sal
Joe
Inspector Lestrade
Policeman
Princess Fatima

The composite setting is -
Sherlock Holmes' rooms at 221b Baker Street
The Hyperian Music Hall stage
The Den of Thieves, Soho
A London street
A wharf in St Katharine's Dock

The year is 1900

MUSIC

Overture

ACT ONE

'There's a story in the Press'	Ensemble
'Elementary, my dear Watson'	Holmes, Watson
'Cousin Bill'	Lily, Chorus
'Ruby's Boy-friends'	Ruby, Chorus
'Here's to beer'	Gang
'Oath of Allegiance'	Gang
'Could I?'	Lily, Chorus

ACT TWO

Overture

'Can-can polka'	Girls
'Could I?'	Lily
'I've visited this Theatre'	Watson, Tilly
'I've sailed the Seven Seas'	Holmes, Gang
'Sauce for the Goose'	Marvo, Chorus
'Oath of Allegiance'	Gang, Holmes
'Lullaby'	Holmes
'Moriarty!'	Moriarty
'I cannot find the word'	Lestrade, Holmes, Watson
'Elementary, my dear Watson'	Ensemble

To
JOHN

SHERLOCK HOLMES IN THE DEERSTALKER
was first presented at the New Windmill Hall, Upminster
on 23rd March, 1984
with the following cast

Dr John Watson	John Jones
Sherlock Holmes	Vivian Leicester
Mrs Hudson	Alison Parkes
Rev. Charles Samuels	Garry Reeves
Alf Barker	Nicholas Hawn
Lily Nightingale	Mary Atkinson
Beth	Jacqui Gray
Tilly	Anna Maria de Pol
Rose	Janine Nicholls
Pearl	Amanda Pitman
Ruby	Brenda Crouch
Marvo	Terence Mustoo
Bob	Graham Turner
Tom	David Curtis
Jim	John Stanford
Old Sal	June Cresswell
Joe	Ian Barry
Inspector Lestrade	Bill Davidson
Policeman	Freddy Woods
Princess Fatima	Alison Barker

Produced by Ian Wilkes

OVERTURE

*[Dr Watson walks out in front of curtain, stepping into the spotlight.
He talks directly to the audience]*

WATSON: *Good evening, ladies and gentlemen, my name is Doctor John
Watson - you may have heard of me - you may have read my stories
serialised in the Strand Magazine of the adventures of Mr Sherlock Holmes,
who has kindly allowed me to chronicle some of his most fascinating cases.
You may have read of the scandal in Bohemia, or puzzled over the five
orange pips, or been frightened by the hound of the Baskervilles (I know I
was), but there is one case which as yet has not been told, a story so
devious and dangerous that I came close to losing my good friend Sherlock
Holmes once again, yet it started so ordinarily. It's a case that I call 'The
Adventure of the Disappearing Princess' or, as some of the so-called popular
press called it, 'Deerstalker'.*

*[Watson retires behind the curtain. Either on to the forestage or into
the auditorium come most of the company singing -]*

THERE'S A STORY IN THE PRESS

CHORUS   There's a story in the press
Which has gained official clearance,
It concerns a young princess
And her sudden disappearance

Now it may mean the start of a royal row
If the girl remains undiscovered,
For somebody must have to find out how
Her guard was left uncovered.

But the hero Holmes will lead
The crime until conclusion,
It'll be his style indeed
To avoid Police intrusion.

For the papers in so many words have said
That the only clue left behind
A deerstalker cap which upon the head
Of Holmes you will often find.

There's a story in the press
Which has gained official clearance,
It concerns a young princess
And her sudden disappearance
And her sudden disappearance
And her sudden disappearance.

[As the Company exit, the curtains rise. To stage right is Sherlock Holmes' room in Baker Street; Stage left is the Den of Thieves in Soho: across the centre of the stage is the Stage of the Hyperian Theatre (see stage plan at back of book). The lights come up on Sherlock Holmes' rooms, where Holmes is intent upon chemical apparatus on a low table by his chair. There is a knock on the door]

HOLMES Yes, what is it, Mrs Hudson?

Mrs HUDSON *[entering]* Sorry to interrupt you, Mr Holmes, but it's Doctor Watson to see you.

HOLMES Oh, that quite all right, show him up.

HUDSON He does that well enough for himself.

HOLMES Come in, my dear friend.

[Doctor Watson comes in]

WATSON Hello, old chap, I just... *[He gives a gentle burp]*

HOLMES Ah, I hear you've been to the Red Lion.

WATSON Yes. But how did you know?

HOLMES Elementary, my dear Watson. That will be all, Mrs Hudson.

HUDSON I doubt that, Mr Holmes, I very much doubt it. I'll be down-stair if you want me. *[Exit]*

HOLMES Are you all right, Watson?

WATSON Yes, never felt better. *[Holmes indicates to Watson to sit down. They both settle into their chairs]*

HOLMES You enjoyed your holiday in Scotland?

WATSON The holiday did me a power of good – and how are you?

HOLMES As a doctor, you should be able to tell me that, better than I could tell you.

WATSON *[laughs]* Oh, good one, Holmes!

HOLMES I hope you brought some of my extra special?

WATSON Oh yes, here you are. *[Hands Holmes a pouch of tobacco]*

HOLMES Thank you. *[Pause while Holmes fills pipe. Then he gets up and saunters over to look through 'window' directly at the audience]* What a strange and devious world we live in. If we could fly out of this window, hand in hand, and hover over this great city, gently remove the roofs and peep in at the queer things that are going on, what plots and machinations would we find hidden behind those shuttered windows, plots stranger than fiction could ever imagine.

WATSON *[joining him at 'window']* But I wager you could work them out with your deductive skills.

HOLMES Maybe. See that little man down there in the street?

WATSON Yes.

HOLMES From here I can tell you he is in trade, works in a small shop

without much light, handles chalk, and does very fine work, although he has a marked lack of imagination.
WATSON   Good gracious, Holmes, how do you work that out?
HOLMES   He's my tailor.   *[Turns away]* Now to the business in hand. *Have you seen 'The Times'?*
WATSON   Of course I have, it's been published for many years. Oh! I see *what you mean - today's 'Times'. No I'm afraid I haven't.* *[Back to seat]*
HOLMES *[pacing round the room]* There's a story that is causing some *excitement in the newspapers. Apparently an Arabian Princess has disappeared.*
WATSON   That must have been what I heard them shouting about in the *street.*
HOLMES   Apparently she had expressed a desire to visit a genuine London *music hall and went to the Hyperian with her guardian, the Reverend Charles Samuels. The place had been surrounded by police as there had been a kidnap threat against her. There'd even been a police Inspector in the auditorium, Inspector Lestrade to be precise.*
WATSON   Well, what happened?
HOLMES   During the show the Princess was asked to help in a magic trick *which involved her being covered in a sheet for but a moment. When it was removed she had vanished and, despite all the police searches, she couldn't be found.*
WATSON   Amazing, but why is it of particular interest to you?
HOLMES   The only clues the police have, Watson, are a deerstalker found *backstage and a description of a tall man wearing a cape-backed overcoat running from the scene of the crime, although how he got past the police no one knows.* *[Stops pacing]*
WATSON   But that description could fit hundreds of people in London.
HOLMES   Certainly, but when you hear it who immediately springs to *mind?*
WATSON   No one I can think of. Oh! It's you, Holmes.
HOLMES   Exactly! And that's what the police may think, so it's up to me *to catch the perpetrator of this crime and prove myself innocent.*
WATSON   If anyone can, you can.
HOLMES   Thank you for your confidence. I see you took a stroll through *Hyde Park this morning.*
WATSON   Yes, but how did you know? *[Rises and joins Holmes at front of stage]*
HOLMES   There are scuff marks on the sole of your boot, which shows *you had to wipe some mud off on the bootscraper. As it has been rather damp lately and the nearest park is Hyde Park and I know your predeliction for feeding the ducks it was an elementary deduction.*
WATSON   You never cease to amaze me, Holmes.

ELEMENTARY, MY DEAR WATSON

HOLMES   *[sings]* Elementary, my dear Watson
                    I seem frequently to say,
                    My powers of deduction

HOLMES

Make things clear as any day.
The shred of cotton on a coat
Or lying on the floor,
May prove of no importance
Or could open up a door.
At every scrap of evidence
You must know how to look,
Until it's so familiar
That you read it like a book,
I cannot tell you how it's done
Or how it all will end,
You see, to me, it's elementary,
My dear friend.

Elementary, my dear Watson,
There, I've said it once again,
The evidence against me
I'm afraid is very plain,
That blessed man Lestrade
Has found, with eyes so keen
A headpiece called a deerstalker
In which I'm often seen.
I'll have to work with all good speed
If I'm to find out who
Would tie me to this devious crime
With such an obvious clue.
I cannot tell you how it's done
Or how it all will end.

WATSON — *I suppose to you it's elementary?*
HOLMES — *Yes, dear friend.*

HOLMES — *Now, Watson, you have chronicled*
My cases all to date

WATSON — *And it's evident I've taken pains*
To get the record straight.

HOLMES — *I hope your publication fees*
Still handsomely compare.

WATSON — *Without your little mysteries*
I'd have no income there.
This latest disappearance
Of a beautiful princess,
You'll find the culprit very soon
I'll drink to your success.

HOLMES — *I cannot tell you how it's done*
Or how it all will end.

WATSON — *I suppose again it's elementary?*
HOLMES — *Yes, dear friend!*

[Watson crosses and stands with back to door. Holmes sits in his chair]
[There is a sound outside the door]

HOLMES   Ah, we have a visitor.

WATSON   No, let me. I think after the years of working with you I should be able to do some deducing myself. Now, let's see. It's a slow, rather timorous step of someone not used to large houses, probably wearing hobnail boots, but with a definite pace of inner confidence. I'd say it was Joe, the bootblack boy. *[Mrs Hudson enters, unseen by Watson, followed by the Rev Charles Samuels]*

HOLMES   Good try, Watson, but actually it's -

HUDSON   - It's the Reverend Charles Samuels.

WATSON   That's amazing, Holmes! You said that without moving your lips and you sounded just like Mrs Hudson!

HOLMES   Come in, Reverend, this is my friend Doctor Watson. Give the gentleman your seat, Watson.

WATSON   What? Oh, I'm sorry... I didn't... Of course, take a seat, sir.

[Samuels takes Watson's chair, Watson stands by mantlepiece]

HUDSON   Will that be all, Mr Holmes? I've got to get back to my cooking.

HOLMES   Yes, thank you very much.

[Mrs Hudson exits]

WATSON   Are you comfortable?

SAMUELS   I make a living.

HOLMES   Now, what can we do for you?

SAMUELS   You have no doubt read about the disappearance of the Princess Fatima and that I am her guardian while she is in this country?

WATSON   Yes, it must be very distressing for you.

HOLMES   If you don't mind my asking, why were you made her guardian? Surely the King would have sent one of his own men.

SAMUELS   Well, he did send a bodyguard, but he wanted her to have a personal companion to show her round while she was over here.

HOLMES   But why you?

SAMUELS   The King and I are old friends. We met while I was a missionary in Arabia. One night while I was staying at his camp I had to return to his tent during the night to pick up some of my books, when I saw a snake about to attack the sleeping King, so I smashed it over the head with the Bible and saved his life. Since then we've been close friends.

HOLMES   The power of the Good Book.

WATSON   That reminds me of a fascinating experience of camp life in Afghanistan.

HOLMES   We don't want to hear about that now, Watson.

WATSON   Sorry.

HOLMES   So you decided to take her to the music hall. Although the place was surrounded by police, why wasn't her bodyguard with her?

SAMUELS   He was ill that night.

HOLMES   I see.

SAMUELS   Despite the warning of a kidnap threat, Princess Fatima insisted on going and the police were guarding us, so it seemed quite safe. When we got there, we watched a number of the acts (jolly good some of them were too) when this magician came on and asked for a member of the audience to assist him. The Princess jumped up and said she would. Half-way through the trick a sheet was thrown over her - only for a moment - but when it was pulled away, she'd disappeared. There was pandemonium, but she couldn't be found anywhere.

HOLMES   Very interesting. You know about the clues the police have found and who some people feel they point to?

SAMUELS   Yes, but I don't listen to idle gossip. I have followed your adventures with great interest and I know of your remarkable skills. By the way, Dr Watson, I think they're very well written.

WATSON   Oh, thank you. We do what we can.

HOLMES   Is there anything else you can tell us that you think may help?

SAMUELS   Not particularly. I think the newspapers have most of the story, but, Mr Holmes, I am very worried about the safety of the Princess. Whoever has her may hurt her, or even kill her, and I couldn't face that.

HOLMES   About those kidnap threats. How did they come to you?

SAMUELS   It was a telephone call to Scotland Yard. I thought it might be a hoax, but... Mr Holmes, if you can find her and save her, I'd be forever in your bedt and so, I'm sure, would King Aziz. Please say you'll help.

HOLMES   I promise I'll do my best.

WATSON   My dear sir, don't worry. If anyone can, Holmes can find her.

SAMUELS   Thank you, gentlemen.

WATSON   Meanwhile I suppose you could pray for her.

SAMUELS   Yes, that's a good idea. I'll pray for us all. [Rises from chair]

WATSON   Can I show you out?

SAMUELS   No, I can find my own way. Thank you, gentlemen. [Exit]

WATSON   Poor gentleman! Well, Holmes, what do we do first?

HOLMES   We are goint to the music hall.

WATSON   That sounds jolly.

HOLMES   We are going to investigate a disappearance. We are not going to enjoy ourselves. [Exeunt]

[The lighting fades on Holmes' room and comes up centre stage (Hyperian Music Hall). Alf Barker is Stage Left, continuing his introductions]

BARKER   ... And now, ladies and gentlemen, I am very proud to announce the little lady you have all been waiting for, that lucious purveyor of loveliness, the girl with the golden larynx, the numero uno chanteuse (that's number one singer to you, sir), the girl with the voice the angels envy, our very own - with a saucy little ditty - ladies and gentlemen, put your hands together for - Lily Nightingale and the Hyperian Girls!

[Barker retires to corner of stage and Lily and the girls run on]

COUSIN BILL

LILY [sings]   I've got a Cousin Alf and I've got a Cousin Fred,
I've another one called Bert, but he's never out of bed,
But the one I hits it off with, call it what you will,
Is me little friend and buddy: me good old Cousin Bill.

LILY

Cousin Bill works on the Great Eastern Railway
He handles all the boxes that come out the luggage cars,
He works so hard, he even carts the mail away
he couldn't be more happy if he thanked his lucky stars.

GIRLS

Now Bill knows Bishopsgate and for his booze he's rarely
late,
He's always the firt down Dirty Dick's Saloon;
He downs a pint at such a rate it makes his tonsils
oscillate,
He's known as Billy Hollow Legs down Dirty Dick's
Saloon!

LILY

Now him and his mate was heaving all the cases out
Stacking them all neat and tidy by the platform side,
Grafting so well, they never heard the starting shout;
The Guv'nor never knew about their little railway ride.

GIRLS

Now Bill knows Bishopsgate, etc.

LILY

When they got back it was well into the afternoon
They couldn't find a Gaffer who would listen to their
tale;
As they both clocked out, someone said 'They're closing
soon!'
You never saw their heels for dust to get a drop of ale!

GIRLS

Now Bill knows Bishopsgate, etc.

[While the song has been going on, Holmes and Watson have entered the auditorium unobtrusively. By the song's end they are at front of stage and applaud]

WATSON   Bravo, bravo!
BARKER   Here, who's that down there? Nobody allowed in during rehearsals. If you want to see the show you've got to pay for your ticket. Now, heave off out of it before I get Harry to throw you out.
WATSON   I'mm Doctor Watson and this is Mr Sherlock Holmes.
BARKER   I don't care if you're King Solomon and he's the Queen of Sheba. Now get out!
HOLMES   Would you mind if I was an Arabian Princess?

[Holmes and Watson climb on to stage]

BARKER   What?
HOLMES   I've been asked to investigate the Princess's disappearance.
BARKER   Not another one! Look, I told the police all I know. Now I've got to get on.
LILY   Don't be so hasty, Alf. Are you really Sherlock Holmes, the famous detective? I've read everything about you.
HOLMES   How very kind.

LILY   Naturally we'll tell you anything you want to know about this case, but I'm afraid we're as much in the dark as everyone else.
BARKER   All right, but I hope it won't take too long – we do have a rehearsal to do. Since the Princess's disappearance we've had to put in an extra performance.
BETH   Sensation seekers, you see.
HOLMES   So this kidnap has actually improved your business.
BARKER   Look I don't go kidnapping girls just to improve my audience.
HOLMES   I never said you did.
PEARL   Wouldn't put it past him.
BARKER   That's not funny.
PEARL   Pardon me for breathing. [Over to Barker]
WATSON   Excuse me, ladies, but we do have some questions.
TILLY [going over to Watson] Of course you do, and you've got such a masterful way about you.
WATSON   Do you think so?
HOLMES   If we may get on.
LILY   Of course, what is it you want to know?
HOLMES   Well, were all of you in the theatre when the disappearance occurred?
LILY   Yes, but we were back stage in our dressing room and didn't see anything.
HOLMES   And you, Mr Barker?
BARKER   I wasn't actually on stage at the time of the disappearance, I was taking a drink of water.
PEARL   Gin more like it.
BARKER   I won't tell you again. Mr Holmes, I know you're only doing your job, but why don't you just go down to Scotland Yard, they've got all our statements.
HOLMES   I like to see the scene of the crime at first hand.
BARKER   Crime? Who said it was a crime?
WATSON   What else could it be?
BARKER   Well, it might be a joke.
WATSON   That's ridiculous!
TILLY [making up to Watson] Do you know, I like a man with a moustache.
WATSON   No, but you hum it and I'll play it! [Laughs – on his own]
HOLMES   Who else was here on the night?
BARKER   Didn't you see the playbill as you came in?
HOLMES   Yes, but remind me.
BARKER   Well, there was Joey Harris, the Menville Sisters, the Flying Zookinis, the Red Blaze, Johnny Wilson the Human Xylophone, the Family Klapp, Orpheus the Magnificent, and, of course, our own Lily Nightingale and the Hyperian Girls – Tilly, Rose, Beth and Pearl.
WATSON   Did you say Orpheus the Magnificent? Do you know, Holmes, he takes a burning piece of cord and sticks it right up –
HOLMES   You didn't mention Marvo the Magician. I believe he was the one who perpetrated the trick. He was here, wasn't he?
PEARL   That goes without saying.

BARKER   So did Tony's Performing Dogs. That's why we had to get rid of them.

HOLMES   Where is he?

PEARL   Who? Tony?

ROSE   No, he means Marvo, don't you, Mr Holmes?

BARKER   At the moment he's helping the police with their enquiries.

WATSON   Good chap.

LILY   I'm sorry, Mr Holmes, if we don't seem to be taking this disappearance too seriously, but it's just the way we theatrical people react to problems – by making light of them. If we can help in any way, of course we will, but I'm afraid it's as much a mystery to us.

HOLMES   It seems that everyone was here, but no one saw anything.

BETH   If you want to find people who saw the show you'd do better to round up that night's audience.

HOLMES   All in good time. Now –

RUBY [entering from backstage] 'Scuse me for interrupting, but I'm off now, Mr Barker.

TILLY   Ruby, you're just in time to meet the great detective, Sherlock Holmes – and Doctor Watson.

RUBY   Pleasure, I'm sure.

HOLMES   Were you here on the night of the disappearance?

RUBY   Yes, but I wasn't on stage, I was just helping one of my boy friends behind the scenes.

BARKER   One of your boy friends! We know all about Ruby's boy friends, don't we, girls?

LILY [to Holmes] Ruby has many boy friends.

RUBY'S BOY FRIENDS

CHORUS   Did you hear about all Ruby's boy-friends?
          It's a story that she will deny;
     For, although she always tries and pree-tends,
          She is never seen without a guy.

RUBY   There is Arthur and there's Donald
     And there's David and there's Ronald,
     There is Tom – to name but just a few.
     Then there's Stephen and there's Mickie
     And there's Allan and there's Dickie
     Not forgetting debonair young Hugh.

CHORUS   Did you hear about all Ruby's boy-friends?   etc....

RUBY   There is Daniel and there's Morris
     And there's Harry and there's Horace
     There is Stan, who gave me such a ball;
     Then there's Andrew and there's Robby
     And there's Walter and there's Bobby –
     And that is all I feel I can recall.

CHORUS   Now you've heard about our Ruby's boy-friends,
                      It's a story now she can't deny,
                For although she always tries and pree-tends,
                      She is never seen without a guy.

ROSE   It only goes to show, doesn't it?
BETH   Yes, that's why she has so many boy friends.
RUBY   I'll give your face such a smack.
HOLMES   Is there anything you can tell me about the Princess?
RUBY   No. Can't I go now. I'm late for my appointment as it is.
ROSE   Who is it this time?
TILLY   Yes, who is your secret admirer?
PEARL   Is he rich?
RUBY   That's for me to know and you to find out.
LILY   Girls, do show some decorum in front of Mr Holmes.
RUBY   All right, but I wish they'd stop picking on me.
BETH   Lady Muck!
LILY   I'm sorry about this, Mr Holmes. Have you any more questions?
HOLMES   Not for Ruby at the moment. I wouldn't want to keep her from
her appointment.
RUBY   Thank you. [Shows her tongue to Beth and exits]
HOLMES   What does Ruby do when she is on stage?
LILY   Juggling, balancing, rolling herself up into a ball, that sort of
thing.
HOLMES   Well, I won't detain you any longer from your rehearsals.
BARKER   You don't want to question the backstage staff?
HOLMES   No, I'm sure they're all honest men, besides, I think you've
alread told me quite a lot.
WATSON   Goodbye, ladies. I must say I enjoyed your dancing very much.
TILLY   Come back to my dressing room and I'll really show you
something.
WATSON   I say, that sounds jolly.
HOLMES   Watson!
WATSON   Of course, what was I thinking of? How silly of me. Can Mr
Holmes come too?
HOLMES   Come along, Watson. [As they start to go, Marvo enters
through the auditorium and comes on stage without noticing Holmes]
LILY   Marvo, are you all right?
MARVO   All night the police kept me. Sixteen hours! But I couldn't tell
them anything. Now I just want to go to bed.
HOLMES   Are you Marvo, inventor of the Triple Coin Penetration?
MARVO   Yes, who are you?
LILY   This is Sherlock Holmes, the famous detective.
TILLY   And this is Doctor Watson.
MARVO   Oh, yes. I've read your stories. I suppose Mr Holmes wants to
ask me a few questions about the disappearance.
HOLMES   I would like to see how the trick was done.
MARVO   I'm tired and a magician doesn't give away his tricks anyway.
Can't it wait?

WATSON   Wait? A girl's life may be in danger.
LILY   Go on, show him, it might help. You don't have to tell him everything, does he, Mr Holmes?
HOLMES   No, he can keep a few tricks up his sleeve, so to speak.
MARVO   All right, but don't expect me to be too good, I'm very tired.
HOLMES   Which trick were you performing?
MARVO   It was that old chestnut, Homesick Jewels. I ask for a member of the audience who has a piece of jewellery – a broach, necklace, or something like that – to come up on stage. I then take the jewel and place it on a tailor's dummy; then the volunteer is covered with a cloth, the jewel vanishes from the dummy with a flash and, when the cloth is pulled off, the jewel is back in place.
WATSON   Amazing, but how's it done?
MARVO   Basically: when the person gives me the jewel I palm it for a clever copy made out of silk and other combustibles.
HOLMES   And it is that which is put on the dummy?
MARVO   Yes. Then when I cover the person with the cloth I put the jewel back on her. The fake is set alight by a small electrical device in the dummy.
HOLMES   But how do you know what jewel to make a copy of?
MARVO   I normally have a confederate in the audience with a fake brooch, but in this case I knew that the Princess was coming and I found a picture of her necklace.
WATSON   So, as well as a magician, you're a skilled pickpocket and forger.
MARVO   What are you implying?
HOLMES   We're implying nothing, we meant professionally.
MARVO   Yes, and I am a professional and I dislike this line of questioning.
HOLMES   And one last question. Did you see the Princess disappear?
MARVO   Not exactly. I'd turned to operate the dummy – I heard a gasp from the audience and turned to see the cloth lying on the floor.
WATSON   The famous unseen trick.
HOLMES   Where exactly was the Princess standing?
MARVO   There, centre stage.
HOLMES   Is there a trapdoor here?   [Examining the stage closely]
MARVO   No. We do have a star trap, but that's over there. [Indicating to the left]
HOLMES   Let's see. Where could she have gone?
WATSON   How about the back curtain?
HOLMES   Good thinking, Watson. [Goes to rear of stage and pushes back curtain] No, there's a solid wall back here. And she couldn't have gone up or to either side or the audience would have seen her.
MARVO   A puzzle as great as the Gordian knot?
HOLMES   May I remind you that Alexander the Great cut the knot with one slash of his sword.
MARVO   This problem won't be so easy.
HOLMES   You think not? Well, we mustn't detain you any longer. [Starts to exit into auditorium]

WATSON   *Ah, this takes me back.*
HOLMES   *Watson, what are you doing?*
WATSON   *It must be being up on stage like this. When I was a young man at University I was a member of the Theatre Club and was quite noted for my eccentric dancing.*
HOLMES   *Watson, don't make a fool of yourself.*
WATSON   *I wonder if I can remember any of it.*

[Watson and Tilly go into a 'Scottish reel'. As it goes on Alf and the girls are amused and join in clapping a beat that increases in pace. Eventually Watson trips over his own feet and crashes down on a small box, about the size of a small suitcase, to the left of the stage, and breaks it]

TILLY   *Are you all right? [Many hands help Watson to his feet]*
WATSON   *I'm dreadfully sorry, I seem to have broken your box.*
HOLMES   *As long as you're all right, old friend...*
BARKER   *Look what you've done; you'll have to pay for that.*
HOLMES   *[looking at the box narrowly] But of course. Will a sovereign cover it?*
BARKER   *Handsomely.*
HOLMES   *As long as I can take it with me.*
BARKER   *Now, hang on, that's music hall property.*
HOLMES   *[handing Barker a coin] But I've just paid you for it.*
BARKER   *But that's not the point.*
LILY   *Let him take it. It's no use to us.*
HOLMES   *[picking up box] Thank you, Miss Nightingale.*
LILY   *Please call me Lily.*
HOLMES   *Goodbye then, Lily, it's been a pleasure meeting you, you've been most helpful. Come along, Watson, we mustn't keep these good people from their work.*
WATSON   *[to Tilly] Goodbye. [to Holmes] I don't see why you had to pay a pound for that old box. [Holmes and Watson exit down stage steps and out through auditorium. Lily gazes after Holmes.]*
BARKER   *Come on, girls, chop chop, we've got rehearsals to get through. I want to go through that dance before the first interval. Be back in ten minutes. [The girls groan and exit. Barker follows slowly]*

[The lights fade on the Hyperian and come up (dimly) on the Den of Thieves, Soho. Old Sal comes on, sits down and starts stirring a caldron of stew; Bob and Tom bring on the table; Ruby enters and stands well in the shadows. After a moment, Jim staggers on. Everyone looks at him]

BOB   *What happened to you, Jim?*
TOM   *You look like you've been dragged through a hedge backwards.*
JIM   *I feel like it. I've just managed to shake off the law.*
BOB   *You haven't been out on a job? You know how the boss feels about that.*
JIM   *But this one was so tempting, Harry and me couldn't resist it.*
TOM   *Yeah, where is Harry?*
JIM   *That's what I'm trying to tell you. We went to knock over Lord Chumley's town house, it being empty as he's up in Scotland for the season.*

TOM   So what happened?
JIM   Well, we got in through the pantry window sweet as a nut and were just working our way to the dining room silver when who should appear in his nightshirt but Lord Chumley himself – and he had a blunderbuss.
BOB   What was he doing back?
JIM   I don't know. Maybe it was raining in Scotland – we didn't hang around to find out. It was down the hall, out the front door, and then we ran straight into the arms of the law. So we done a runner down the main road and I managed to jump on the back of a passing carriage.
TOM   What about Harry?
JIM   He tried to run down an alleyway. He tried to leap a wall topped with sharp spikes.
TOM   So what happened?
JIM   He was caught by the peelers. *[The others all wince]*
BOB   Well, that's Harry gone, I don't know what the boss is going to say.
TOM   You're always worrying about what the boss will say. I wonder what the boss is going to do. All he seems to do now is have us sitting round here and waiting.
RUBY *[coming forward]* You lot are always moaning. Here we are on the greatest job ever conceived by a great criminal mind and you're moaning. Aren't they, Sal?
SAL   I heard that!
BOB   Poor old Sal, deaf as a post.
SAL   What?
BOB   I said 'you're as deaf as a post'.
SAL   This ain't toast, it's soup, you fool. *[Hits him with her ladle]*
JIM   I think she's the only entertainment we've got around here.
RUBY   What are you talking about: the boss lays on good food and good beer.
JIM   And good song.
RUBY   Yes, so what are you lot griping about? *[Picks up jug of beer and pours some into each of their mugs]* Eat, drink and be merry, for to-morrow we get stinking rich.

HERE'S TO BEER

GANG *[in unison]* Now beer is a pastime that most of us last time
                    Decided we'd next time resist;
                    But barrels are piling and glasses are smiling
                    And Ruby tells us what we've missed.
                    With barrels reclining and us all declining
                    To take but one small extra drink;
                    We're none of us braggin' that we're on the wagon
                    For what would our Boss of us think?

Chorus   Here's to beer! Here's to beer!
                    Here's to beer that is strong, cool and clear,
                    There's brown and there's bitter and mild and there's stout,

And anything else you can think of, just shout!
For there's beer! Here's to beer!
The Boss is providing and we're all imbibing
The beer that will give us good cheer!

We're all in this willing to make just a shilling
When all of the work has been done;
We'll never believe that the Boss can't conceive
That we're all of us still on the run.
But soon when we're laid off and finally paid off
We'll all go back on to the lag;
So now the advice is let's use our devices
And don't leave our spirits to sag!

Chorus   Here's to beer! etc.

TOM   Very good, Ruby, now come and sit on my knee.
RUBY   Not on <u>your</u> knee, but anyway we've got work to do.

[The gang groan]

JIM   What is it now?
RUBY   I know all work and no play makes Jack very happy, but if
we're going to pull off this job successfully, we've got to put our backs into
it.
SAL   But that would ruin the soup!
RUBY   As you know, stages one and two of the plan are completed.
BOB   So what do we do now?
RUBY   I'll let the Boss tell you in person. *[Goes to curtain at rear]*
And now, ladies and gentlemen, I give you - the Boss! *[Pulls a cord that
opens curtain to reveal a gramophone horn through which the voice will
come]*
VOICE   This is the voice of your Leader.
SAL   Hello, Boss.
VOICE   As you know, the first two parts of this operation have been
successful - for which I congratulate you.
BOB   Thanks, Boss.
VOICE   Part three is about to begin, but before I get on to that, I
believe someone has not been following the rules. *[Pause, while gang
exchange nervous glances]* The miscreant will now stand up. *[No one moves]*
I am disappointed in you. Jim, forward. *[Jim rises]* You went on a
personal job with Harry and Harry got caught.
BOB   Yeah, by the peelers.
JIM   I'm sorry, Boss. It won't happen again.
VOICE   But what if Harry talks? You have endangered the whole project
BOB   I'm sure he won't talk, he's a good man.
VOICE   Maybe, but there must be punishment for this flagrant dis-
obedience.
JIM   It won't happen again.
VOICE   Close your eyes and turn round. *[Jim does so]* And now the
punishment will be carried out.

[*Ruby walks behind Jim and puts a pistol to the back of his neck. When she pulls the trigger there is a loud explosion and Jim falls prone. After a moment he comes cautiously back to life and feels himself all over and then rises shakily to his feet*]

JIM   But I'm not dead.
RUBY   Not this time, next time it won't be a blank.
VOICE   And now to more important matters. I have decided that the best way to ensure your loyalty is to have you swear.
TOM   I do that all the time.
VOICE   You must swear allegiance to me, blind unquestioning obedience.

OATH OF ALLEGIANCE

GANG

Now an oath we'll swear
To a Boss who's fair,
Though he keeps us waiting
With his love of cogitating /
From the right we'll dress
Then we'll all say yes,
To the oath of stern allegiance
And we'll never bear a grievance, /
No we'll never bear a grievance
On our oath of stern allegiance,
And we'll never question orders
While the Boss repels the boarders,
      For we always keep the oaths we swear!

Now we're on this job
For this guv'nor nob,
And it's not confusing
Though it might seem quite amusing, /
For we're all tea-leaves,
Which is slang for thieves,
But we've sworn our own allegiance
And we'll never bear a grievance, /
No, we'll never bear a grievance
When we've sworn our own allegiance,
And we'll never question orders
While the Boss repels the boarders,
      For we always keep the oaths we swear!

[*very fast*]

Now an oath we've sworn
To a Boss care-worn,
Who has kept us waiting
With his love of cogitating,
But we must impress
For we all said 'yes'
To the oath of stern allegiance
And we'll never bear a grievance

> No we'll never bear a brievance
> To our oath of stern allegiance
> And we'll never question orders
> While the Boss repels the boarders, /
> For we always keep the oaths we swear!

[At end of song, exit Sal]

VOICE Good. Now to work. You will be pleased to know that stage three has already begun.
BOB What do you want us to do?
VOICE For the moment, I just want you to wait.
TOM I told you.
VOICE Do not worry. There will be plenty of work for you to do when the time comes, then we will be going on a little sea voyage.
JIM But I get seasick
VOICE Anyone who cannot come will be dealt with.
JIM I always said I was looking forward to a boat trip.
VOICE Now, my little ones, we will soon have evrything we wish – and more.
RUBY That's what I told them. We should be very grateful.
BOB Yes, and we are, Boss.
VOICE And one last thing.
BOB Yes, Boss?
VOICE Stop calling me Boss.
BOB Yes, Boss, sorry.
VOICE Don't aplogise, that's a sign of weakness.
BOB Sorry, Bo –
RUBY Be quiet. We're soon to be very rich because of our leader, let's hear it for our leader.
BOB Three cheers for our leader. Hip, hip...

[The gang give three ragged cheers, then exit with Ruby. The lighs go down on the Den of Thieves and rise on Sherlock Holmes' room. Holmes is examining the box he took from the Hyperian with a magnifying glass. There is a knock: Holmes puts down his experiments]

HOLMES Yes? Who is it?
LILY *[off]* It's me. Lily Nightingale from the Hyperian.
HOLMES Oh, yes. *[Quickly tidies the table, straightens his own clothes and smooths his hair]* Do come in.
LILY *[entering]* I had to show myself up. Mrs Hudson said she had something in the oven.
HOLMES Do sit down.
LILY I can't stop long. *[Sits in Holmes' chair]*
HOLMES To what do I owe this visit? I thought you'd told me everything at the music hall.
LILY Well, to be honest, Mr Holmes – or may I call you Sherlock?
HOLMES Whatever you wish.
LILY Well, Sherlock, there is something I wanted to tell you, but with

all the girls around and Mr Barker, I wasn't sure if I could talk in front of them.
HOLMES   Was it something embarrassing?
LILY   Oh no, nothing like that, but with everyone around I just didn't want too many questions to be asked.
HOLMES   I see. What was it?
LILY   Do you live here on your own? *[Rises, goes to mantlepiece]*
HOLMES   Was that what you wanted to ask?
LILY   No, I was just wondering. I mean, I've always thought you needed a woman's touch around the home.
HOLMES   I have Mrs Hudson who cleans up once in a while, and I have Dr Watson for company.
LILY   But surely you must have lots of women friends?
HOLMES   I don't see where this line of questioning is leading us.
LILY   I'm sorry, I've embarrassed you.
HOLMES   Certainly not, I appreciate your concern. But really I would like to know why you came here.
LILY   Well, it was on the night of the disappearance. I told you I was in the dressing room.
HOLMES   Yes, with the other girls.
LILY   You see I was...*[Knocks a test-tube from mantlepiece into fireplace]* Oh, I'm terribly sorry.
HOLMES   That's all right. It was empty.
LILY   Doing some experiments?
HOLMES   Yes, it's one of my pastimes. I like to know what things really are.
LILY   Isn't that the old box that you bought at thhe music hall?
HOLMES   Yes, I noticed an interesting stain on the lid. I haven't ascertained what it is yet.
LILY   But why? It's just a silly old box.
HOLMES   Whhen I see something that interests me, I like to know all about it.
LILY   Does that include people?
HOLMES   We appear to have strayed from the point.
LILY   I'm very sorry, I've always been like this, easily sidetracked. Some people say it's my theatrical blood.
HOLMES   How long have you been in the profession?
LILY   For as long as I can remember. I was born in a trunk, as they say. My mother and father had a tumbling act. They worked very hard for a pittance. They were often 'resting', so I learnt what hardship was. I vowed i'd never be poor, like them, but have enough money to live life as it should be lived – to the full. I'm sorry, Sherlock, you don't want to hear my problems.
HOLMES   You're not boring me, but you did say you came to tell me something about the disappearance.
LILY   Well, I was in the dressing room with the other girls and we heard a commotion – that must have been when the Princess vanished. I was sitting nearest to the door and I heard the footsteps of someone running.

HOLMES   Is that so surprising? Surely it was someone running to see what had happened.
LILY   That's the point. The feet were running in the wrong direction, towards the stage door.
HOLMES   How can you be sure of the direction?
LILY   I've worked at the Hyperian for quite a time and you get used to the echoes.
HOLMES   But if you're right how could he - orr she - have got past the police?
LILY   I don't know, I can only tell you what I heard.
HOLMES   This is very interesting, but I still can't see why you couldn't tell me about this in front of the others.
LILY   Excuse me, Sherlock, but I wonder if I could go and wash my hands?
HOLMES   Yes - but I don't see why you didn't tell me this at the music hall.
LILY   I'd still like to wash my hands.
HOLMES   Oh, I see! I'm dreadfully sorry. It's straight through there on your left. [Indicates the bedroom exit]
LILY   Thank you kindly. [Exit]
HOLMES   [to himself] Most interesting. [Stands indecisively for a moment then picks up box, scrapes something off lid with a scalpel. He puts this into a test tube and adds a liquid, shaking them up] I shall have to find out what that stain is.
LILY [re-entering] Thank you, Sherlock, I'm sorry to have taken up so much of your time.
HOLMES   No, it was my pleasure, but you don't have to rush away, do you? I was very interested to hear about your parents. Are they still alive?
LILY   No. My mother was run down by a horse omnibus and my father died while attempting a triple back somersault.
HOLMES   What happened?
LILY   He missed the stage and landed in the kettle drum. He always wanted to go out with a bang. I'm sorry, Sherlock, you see what I mean about us theatricals making light of problems and disasters.
HOLMES   I'm sorry, but there's one other thing I want to ask you about the Princess's disappearance.
LILY   I'd like to talk, Sherlock, but I really must be getting back to the theatre, we've got two performances tonight - as we have every night.
HOLMES   But this will only take a minute.
LILY   A minute's what I haven't got, but it's been a lovely experience talking to you.
HOLMES   This might sound strange coming from me, but it has been a true pleasure conversing with you, Miss Nightingale.
LILY   Goodbye [She kisses Holmes on the cheek. He is stunned into silence] I'll see myself out.
HOLMES   Oh, no! Allow me to show you to the door. [Exeunt]

[The lights fade down on Holmes' rooms and come up on the Hyperian stage. The girls enter casually]

PEARL   *... and the monkey said to the organ grinder "If that's what he does for sixpence, I'm glad I didn't give him a shilling."*

[The girls break into shrill laughter]

ROSE   *That was a good one.*
BETH   *As the bishop said to the actress.*

[The girls all laugh hysterically again]

TILLY   *Well, at least we're all in a good mood.*
ROSE   *Why shouldn't we be with the money we're going to get.*
TILLY   *It's not going to be that much.*
BETH   *Don't be such a sour puss.*
TILLY   *But I can't help feeling worried.*
PEARL   *Don't be so silly, Tilly, soon you'll be spending willy nilly.*
ROSE   *Sounds like she's been at the cooking sherry again.*

[Pearl blows her a raspberry]

BETH   *I think I'll buy myself one of those great big hats with all the vegetable salad on it – and a coach and four.*
TILLY   *Do be quiet.*
BETH   *Who's to hear us?*

[Enter Lily. The other girls crowd round her]

TILLY   *Lily! How did it go with you-know-who?*
LILY   *It was very interesting.*
BETH   *Interesting?*
LILY   *Yes, he's a very nice man; very considerate.*
PEARL   *If a little strange. [Laughs]*
LILY   *There was nothing like that. In fact, we got on quite well.*
BETH   *Not 'arf.*
LILY   *I think I could get to like him, like him quite a lot, in fact. Mr Sherlock Holmes is a very impressive man.*
BETH   *I think she's got a touch of the sun.*
TILLY   *In this weather?*
BETH   *Well, a touch of the cold then.*
TILLY   *Could you be serious for a minute?*
BETH   *Anyone got a watch?*
TILLY   *Did you really like him?*
LILY   *I think so. He's the sort of man that if you got to know him really well, you might be able to fall in love with him.*
ROSE   *But, Lily, he's a well-known masser... masso... massi... well, you know, he doesn't like women.*
LILY   *I wouldn't be so sure about that.*
PEARL   *Ooh!*
TILLY   *Do you think... Do you think you could get to love him?*
LILY   *I don't know.*

COULD I?

[sings]   Could I this man of science sway
And tempt him turn his head my way,
To leave his world and then I'd say;

19

LILY   *My heart is set a'fire.*
GIRLS   *Her heart is set a'fire.*
LILY   *Could I this man of method take*
And deep within his soul awake
A spirit which will work forsake;
This man whom I admire.
GIRLS   *This man whom she'll admire.*
LILY   *Could I then take this man for mine,*
As part of heaven's grand design
And surely, just as sun will shine
Of him I'd never tire.
GIRLS   *Of him she'd never tire.*

[Enter Alf Barker]

BARKER   What do you girls think you're doing, sitting about like this?
TILLY   We were just trying out a new song.
BARKER   I thought I hadn't heard it before.
LILY   Did you like it, Mr Barker?
BARKER   Yes I did and, more importantly, I think the customers will enjoy it. They like that romantic stuff, especially the way you put it over. We'll have it for the show tonight. Can you have it ready in time?
LILY   I should think so.
BARKER   Come on then, girls. We have a show to put on. Move your pretty little backsides backstage before we open the doors.
PEARL   Cheeky.

[The girls start to wander off, chatting amongst themselves]

BARKER   I don't know what the place is coming to. Come on, girls, hurry along, we haven't got all day. *[Exeunt]*

[The lights fade down on the Hyperian and come up on Holmes' rooms. Mrs Hudson is busy with a feather duster. Enter Holmes]

HUDSON   Oh, I didn't expect you back so soon, Mr Holmes.
HOLMES   I've got some experiments to finish. Could you tidy up later?
HUDSON   Of course, Mr Holmes. *[Exit]*

[Holmes picks up music hall box and examines it with magnifying glass. There is a knock. Holmes puts down box, goes to door and opens it. Enter Watson]

WATSON   I hope I'm not interrupting anything.
HOLMES   No.
WATSON   Now, how are we getting along with the investigation?
HOLMES   The investigation. If I'm not mistaken – and I very rarely am – we have seen a number of scarlet fish.
WATSON   Scarlet fish?
HOLMES   Red herrings, me dear fellow. Consider it, a magician with a classical education, people who are very willing to talk to us yet tell us nothing.
WATSON   And what about Lily Nightingale?

HOLMES   A fascinating woman. Watson, I have the feeling that this matter is more devious than we first imagined. We will have to tread very carefully in this case, Watson.
WATSON   Case? You mean this ole box?
HOLMES   No, I meant the investigation. But this old box is of interest. [Picks box up] You see this stain on the inside of the lid?
WATSON   Yes.
HOLMES   I've run some experiments on it and it proves to be greasepaint of a common brand used by theatricals.
WATSON   They must use lots of that stuff at the music hall, so it's another dead end.
HOLMES   Maybe, maybe not. I'd like you to notice... [There is a knock] Come in, Mrs Hudson.
[Mrs Hudson enters with Joe, the bootblack boy, who has obviously been specially cleaned for the occasion]
HUDSON   Excuse me, Mr Holmes, but this article says he has a package for you.
HOLMES   Why, it's Joe the bootblack boy.
HUDSON   Is it? Well, I never. I didn't recognise you with your face all clean like that.
JOE   I always clean meself up when I'm going to meet the great Sherlock Holmes.
HOLMES [to Watson] Here's one who hasn't read your stories.
JOE   No, I can't read; but my big brother reads them to me from back copies of the Strand Magazine. Cor, they are exciting.
HOLMES   Well, Joe, what have you brought me?
JOE   A lady gave me this bowl of eggs to give to you and said you'd give me half a crown for them. [Hands Holmes a china bowl]
WATSON   Sounds like a cheeky way of selling eggs to me.
HOLMES   Who gave them to you?
JOE   She said I wasn't to say.
HOLMES   I won't ask you to break your confidence. Here's half a sovereign for the eggs. [Tosses Joe a coin]
JOE   Cor, thanks, Mr Holmes, you're a toff.
HOLMES   Spend it wisely.
JOE   I will. [Runs out past Mrs Hudson]
HUDSON   I don't know what the younger generation is coming to. I'll be downstairs if you want me. [Exit]
WATSON   A half sovereign for a box of eggs! You must have money to burn.
HOLMES   Not if I'm not mistaken.
WATSON   And you very rarely are.
HOLMES   One of these eggs will contain the information we require.
WATSON   How do you mean?
HOLMES   There's an old trick with which you can write on the inside of an egg. What you do is dissolve an ounce of alum with a half pint of vinegar; then you take this and, using it as ink, write on the shell of an egg with a pointed brush. Then all you do is boil the egg for fifteen minutes and

the lettering disappears from the shell. But - and here's the clever part - when you break the egg open the message appears on the hardboiled white.

WATSON   Fantastic. You mean all we have to do is crack open the egg [Selects an egg from the bowl] and we get the message? [Breaks the raw egg, which runs all over his hands]   Yuk!

HOLMES   You'd best wash your hands in the other room while I find the right egg.

WATSON   Yes, old chap. Sorry. [Exit into bedroom]

HOLMES   Now, let's see. [He spins a number of eggs to find which one is hard boiled: he finds it] This seems to be the little beauty.

[Watson screams in the bedroom and then enters his face full of fear. There is a small snake on his shoulder]

WATSON   Holmes!

HOLMES   Stay perfectly still, old chap, don't move a muscle. [Goes slowly to the fireplace and picks up the poker; then springs across the room and knocks the snake from Watson's shoulder. When it is on the ground he kills it with two swift blows]

WATSON   [shakily] Thanks, old man, you saved my life.

HOLMES   Think nothing of it, but you're lucky, one bite from that animal could mean death.

WATSON   But whoever put it there must have meant it for you. Do you think someone's trying to kill you?

HOLMES   No. Whoever left that here meant it as a calling card to let me know that they knew I was on to them and that they know a lot about me.

WATSON   What do you mean? It could have killed you.

HOLMES   Not so. You remember my trip up the Amazon a couple of months ago?

WATSON   Yes.

HOLMES   I was bitten by a similar snake. Luckily I was given the antidote in time and its effects should still be active. Whoever planted this know me very well.

WATSON   But who could have put it there?

HOLMES   I'll get to that in a minute, but first to the egg. [He carefully cracks and peels the egg]   There we are: the message. 'Your answer lies in the Den of Thieves in Soho. P.S. Beware of snake.' [Holmes and Watson look at each other]

WATSON   Amazing! And this is just an ordinary egg. [Takes egg from Holmes and bites it. The alum dries his mouth] Oh!

HOLMES   Yes, alum is a nasty taste, someone must have used a bit too much.

WATSON [with dry mouth and pursed lips] What'll I do?

[There is a knock at the door]

HOLMES   Do come in, Inspector Lestrade.

[Enter Lestrade, followed by Mrs Hudson]

HUDSON   Wipe your feet before you come in. I don't know, this place is getting like Piccadilly Circus, what with people popping in and popping out. Now don't keep Mr Holmes too long, he's a busy man.

HOLMES   Thank you, Mrs Hudson.
[Exit Mrs Hudson]
WATSON   Hello, Lestrade.
HOLMES   You'd best go into the other room and have a drink of water to get rid of that.
WATSON   Yes, excuse me. [Exits into bedroom]
LESTRADE   What's the matter with him?
HOLMES   Dry mouth. Now, you've come to ask me some questions about the Princess's disappearance.
LESTRADE   Yes. Great Scotland Yard! What's that dead snake doing on the floor?
HOLMES   If it's dead – nothing. About the Princess?
LESTRADE   The Chief has put me in charge of the case.
HOLMES   I understand she disappeared in front of your eyes.
LESTRADE   Yes. And even though I saw it I still can't believe it. I mean, people don't just disappear into thin air. It's a puzzle.
HOLMES   But every puzzle has a solution, Lestrade.
LESTRADE   That's what the Chief thinks; that's why he's asked me to bring you in for questioning.
WATSON [entering] You can't seriously think that Holmes would have perpetrated such a crime?
LESTRADE   I don't, but we must investigate every avenue. There is the fact that the description fitted Mr Holmes – and the deerstalker.
HOLMES   But I have my deerstalker here.
LESTRADE   You could have bought another one.
WATSON   Ridiculous. Anyone can wear a deerstalker. Hats like that are ten a penny.
HOLMES   Hardly, Watson, but we take your point.
LESTRADE   Look, Mr Holmes, I've worked with you on many occasions and I know you wouldn't be involved in such a crime – in fact, you're about one of the best men I've ever met, but I've still got to take you in. Just for questioning, you understand.
WATSON   If you know he's innocent, why waste your time questioning Mr Holmes, instead of going out and catching the real criminals?
LESTRADE   I'd love to, but orders is orders.
WATSON   Take one step nearer and I'll punch you on the nose.
LESTRADE   Are you threatening an Officer?
HOLMES   Gentlemen, gentlemen. I understand your feelings, but, as Inspector Lestrade says, orders is orders. I'll be happy to accompany you to the Station. I'm sure it won't take long, will it?
LESTRADE   Oh no, sir, a mere formality.
WATSON   Seems a bally waste of time, if you ask me.
HOLMES   I've heard, Lestrade, that you might be up for promotion.
LESTRADE   We lives in hopes.
HOLMES   I'm sorry. I wonder if I could fetch my pipe, it's in the other room.
LESTRADE   Of course, Mr Holmes.

[Holmes exits into bedroom]

WATSON   I think you're being very silly, Lestrade.
LESTRADE Don't go on about it. You don't think I like doing it? Hey, isn't this Mr Holmes' pipe on the mantlepiece. Mr Holmes?

[As Lestrade goes towards bedroom, there is a crash of breaking glass. Lestrade runs into bedroom and returns after a short pause]

LESTRADE He's done a runner. Mr Holmes leapt out of the window. This looks very bad for him - but we'll get him!
WATSON   No you don't, Lestrade!

[As Lestrade runs to the door, Watson grabs him by the leg. During the next few speeches Lestrade drags Watson slowly across the stage]

LESTRADE Let go of me, you fool. You're only making it worse.
WATSON   I won't let you get him.
LESTRADE Let go of me. Let go of my leg. Gerroff. [Lestrade frees himself] I'll get him if it's the last thing I do, as sure as my name's George Lestrade. [Exit]
WATSON [climbing painfully to his feet] Oh dear, what could have happened? He must have a good reason for it. But I can't believe it, Sherlock Holmes on the run!

CURTAIN

ACT TWO

OVERTURE

[Dr Watson comes in front of the curtain, into a spotlight, and talks directly to the audience]

WATSON   Ah, there you are. As you will remember, the case has reached a worrying point with Sherlock Holmes disappearing like that and Lestrade and the whole of the London constabulary after him. I told Lestrade he was wasting his time, but he wouldn't listen. I'm certain Holmes has a good reason for what he did – but I, for one, can't think of it. And then there's the poor Princess – people seem to have forgotten her in all the excitement. It's all very worrying, very worrying indeed. I've got to do something – I know! I'll go to the Hyperian Music Hall; I might find some clues there and, if not, it will take my mind off things. They've got some very good acts: excuse me.

[Watson goes to the left of the stage and the curtains open. As they do, the Girls come on and perform a lively can-can polka. When they finish Watson joins in the applause as a member of the audience. The Girls exit, Alf Barker enters]

BARKER   Thank you, the Hyperian Girls. Weren't they lovely, ladies and gentlemen. And now we have my favourite and your favourite, the delectable Miss Lily Nightingale!

[Exit Barker, enter from the opposite side Lily, who comes to centre stage]

COULD I?

LILY   Could I this man of science sway,
And tempt him turn his head my way,
To leave his world and then I'd say:
    My heart if set afire.
Could I this man of method take
And deep within his heart awake,
A spirit which will work forsake:
    This man whom I admire.
Could I then take this man for mine,
As part of heaven's grand design
And surely just as sun will shine;
    Of him I'd never tire.

O, love of loves now hear the prayer
I whisper on the still night air,
Speeding 'neath the star-lit vault

> Your heart to seek and softy court
> For you undying love I'll swear
> O, love now hear my prayer.

[Re-enter Alf Barker as Lily's applause dies down]

BARKER   Wasn't that beautiful? And now something which I know some of you have been waiting for all evening - I am proud to present the Hyperian's famous and celebrated - interval!

[As the stage lights dim, Barker exits and Lily walks over to Dr Watson in his corner in the 'audience'. He is deep in thought]

LILY   A penny for them?

WATSON   What? Oh, I am sorry. I was miles away. Can I get you a drink?

LILY   Not while I'm working.

WATSON   Good girl.

LILY   Are you still worried about Sherlock's disappearance?

WATSON   Yes: I'm sure he had a reason and that he isn't guilty, or anything, but it still worries me.

LILY   I understand.

WATSON   I enjoyed that song you just sang, but to tell you the truth, one of my reasons for coming here tonight was to see if I could find any clues about the disappearance of the Princess. I don't suppose you could tell me anything more?

LILY   I only wish I could.

WATSON   I can't stop worrying about Holmes.

LILY   Well, if there's anything I can do for you, just ask.

WATSON   Thank you.

LILY   In my short meeting with Sherlock, I found him a very impressive man.

[Enter Tilly]

TILLY   There you are, Lily. Oh, Doctor Watson.

WATSON   Hello, Tilly.

TILLY   Lily, it's almost time to get ready for Act Two.

LILY   Yes, I won't be long. *[To Watson]* I've got this awkward costume to put on and it takes simply ages. I wonder if you'll excuse me, please. *[Exit]*

TILLY   Did you see our dance, Doctor Watson?

WATSON   Yes, but I didn't enjoy it as much -

TILLY   Wasn't it up to standard?

WATSON   It isn't that, it's just that I can't concentrate.

TILLY   If there's anything I can do?

I'VE VISITED THIS THEATRE

WATSON   I've visited this theatre
        To see what else is new.

TILLY   Have you worked a theory out?

WATSON   I cannot find a clue.
So now it's back to Baker Street
        Where Holmes first took to flight,

                    I'd better make a note of things
                        In case Lestrade was right.

                    The case that he's embarked upon
                        Is really rather strange,
                    Lestrade's convinced he's part of it,
                        A view he will not change.
                    I own it looks peculiar
                        That Holmes should choose to run,
                        For if all things are equal
                        Then crime he has not done.

TILLY   Now Holmes is Holmes and that's a fact
                        You'll have to build from there.
WATSON   I have no notion where he's gone.
TILLY   There's some who do not care.
WATSON   If past performance is a guide
                        We'll have to sit and wait
                    For Holmes to turn up once again
                        And set the record straight.

WATSON   I think I'd better get off home now.
TILLY   Good-bye. *[As he turns to go, she kisses him on the fore-head. Tilly exits and the lights go down on the Hyperian and up on the forestage area that represents the outside of 221b Baker Street. Lestrade emerges from the door of 221b and intercepts Watson mid-stage]*
LESTRADE   Doctor Watson, I presume?
WATSON   Lestrade.
LESTRADE   I was hoping I'd run into you.
WATSON   Strange; my thoughts were completely different.
LESTRADE   Now look, Doctor Watson, you know I'm only doing my job.
WATSON   That's what they all say.
LESTRADE   You must admit Mr Holmes's running away was suspicious, jumping out of the window like that.
WATSON   He must have hhad a good reason.
LESTRADE   Well, we'll get him, whatever it was, and if you have any information which could lead to his apprehension I would suggest you let us know – keeping facts from the police is a criminal offence, you know.
WATSON   I only wish I did know something – then I could enjoy myself by not telling you!
LESTRADE   Don't take that tone. You're lucky I didn't arrest you for assaulting an Officer in the course of his duty.
WATSON   I've told you before that you'd do better looking for whoever kidnapped the Princess.
LESTRADE   What makes you think we aren't?
WATSON   You bounder! *[Springs into an exaggerated boxing pose: Lestrade responds. They face each other unmoving for a moment]*
LESTRADE   Try it and I'll run you in. It's only our past friendship which stopped me from taking you in for questioning. If you do hear anything,

you'd best let me know. You know where you can contact me. *[Exit]*
WATSON   Impudent fellow! *[As Watson reaches the door of 221b, it opens and Mrs Hudson, dressed for walking and with a shopping basket, appears. Watson, not noticing her, goes to knock on her face, but just stops himself in time]*
HUDSON   Doctor Watson!
WATSON   Oh, hello, Mrs Hudson.
HUDSON   Good afternoon, Doctor Watson. I'm just going out to do some shopping. That Inspector Lestrade was round her a few minutes ago casting aspersions on Mr Holmes - very unlike him.
WATSON   He seems to think that Holmes was in on the disappearance of that Princess.
HUDSON   I know. I told him it was absurd. But I do wish I knew what had happened to Mr Holmes. I do get awfully worried, the thought of him out there somewhere.
WATSON   I'm sure that wherever he is he can take care of himself and that we'll hear from him soon. Meanwhile, I've just popped round to collect a few things.
HUDSON   You can let yourself out. *[She exits across the stage]*
WATSON   Poor lady! *[Goes through front door. Lights come up on Holmes' rooms. Inside there is a scruffily-dressed seaman looking at some papers on Holmes' desk (It is, of course, Holmes in a brilliant disguise!). As Watson enters the room, the lights on the street go down]*
WATSON   I say, you bounder, leave Holmes' things alone. *[He grapples with the 'stranger', who submits almost without a struggle]*
HOLMES   It's a fair cop, guv'nor, please don't report me to the coppers, I've got a wife and ten children to support. I was desperate: say you won't report me.
WATSON   Indeed I will report you. Trying to make off with the belongings of the great Sherlock Holmes.
HOLMES   The great Sherlock Holmes! Cor, if I'd realised this was his place, I'd never have broken in. I'm a great follower of his. I've read all the stories written by that brilliant author Doctor Watson. Here, you're not him, are you?
WATSON   I have that honour.
HOLMES   Let me shake you by the hand. 'Course, we have met before.
WATSON   Met before? I wouldn't be seen dead with a vagabond like you - unless it was on one of our criminal cases.
HOLMES   Surely you remember me?
WATSON   Can't say I do.
HOLMES   But surely you must. *[Removes hat]* It's elementary, my dear Watson.
WATSON   I assure you I don't. *[Double takes]* You're not - you can't be - is it you, Holmes?
HOLMES   I certainly hope so!
WATSON   Holmes, my dear chap! *[Embraces Holmes, then realising, pulls himself together]* Nice to see you again. Mrs Hudson was getting quite worried. I, of course, knew you'd be back.

HOLMES   Of course. I'm glad the disguise worked.
WATSON   But why the escape?
HOLMES   I knew if I had gone with Lestrade that would have taken time and, in this case, time is of the essence and I could afford to lose any of that vital commodity.
WATSON   But why the disguise?
HOLMES   You remember the egg?
WATSON   I can't forget it.
HOLMES   That said that our answer lies in the den of thieves in Soho, so I have donned a suitable disguise in the hope that I will be accepted amongst them and will be able to foil their plot.
WATSON   Good thinking, but there must be hundreds of dens of thieves in Soho.
HOLMES   But remember that on the egg it said 'the den of thieves' – that would suggest that it was the name of a specific place.
WATSON   You mean like a pub?
HOLMES   Hardly, but some commonly-known meeting point of London's low life.
WATSON   I see. But how are you going to find it?
HOLMES   I'll have to put it about that I'm looking for some criminal work and hope that will lead me to the right place.
WATSON   You'd best be careful, old chap.
[Enter Mrs Hudson, who is taken aback for a second, then runs over to Holmes]
HUDSON   Oh, Mr Holmes, thank goodness you're back safe and sound.
HOLMES   Thank you, Mrs Hudson.
WATSON   You recognised him?
HUDSON   Of course I did, I'm used to all his disguises.
WATSON   So am I: didn't fool me for a minute – well, perhaps a minute.
HUDSON   Would you like something to eat?
HOLMES   I'd love to, but I really have to be going.
HUDSON   Already? But where are you going?
HOLMES   I can't tell you exactly, but if I'm right –
WATSON   And you usually are.
HOLMES   – it should be where the Princess Fatima is.
HUDSON   Do take care.
WATSON   What if you run into trouble?
HOLMES   If I do, I'll try to get a message to you so you can help me out. In the meantime, I want you both to keep my re-appearance a secret and behave as if I am still missing.
WATSON   Glad to. Now I have got something to keep from Inspector Lestrade.
HOLMES   Good-bye, dear friends. *[Shakes hands with Watson and exits]*
WATSON   'Bye, old chap. Gad, he's a brave man.
HUDSON   He certainly is. Now. I've got some angel cakes: would you like some with your tea?
WATSON   Rather!

[They exit. The lights go down on Holmes' rooms and come up on the street scene. There are a couple of roughs lounging around, as is Ruby. One of the roughs (who could be Jim from the Gang) wanders across as Holmes enters and brushes against him]

HOLMES   Hey, you.
TOUGH   Yeah, what d'you want?
HOLMES   I'm a seaman not long in port and I've heard a whisper there's some easy money to be made round here.
TOUGH   Money's never easy to come by.
HOLMES   Maybe you ain't looking in the right places. I'm looking for the den of thieves, if you know what I mean?
ROUGH   You calling me stupid?
HOLMES   That all depends.
ROUGH   You asking for a thick ear?
HOLMES   Forget it. I've killed a man and I ain't too worried about doing it again. Get the message?
ROUGH   Suit yourself. I've got more important things to do. *[Exit]*

[Ruby saunters over to Holmes]

RUBY   Hey, Mister, did I hear you say you're looking for easy money?
HOLMES   I'm looking to get it – not spend it.
RUBY   Don't be like that, Mister, we could make a deal.
HOLMES   What sort of a deal?
RUBY   I heard you mention the den of thieves. It just so happens that I know where it is.
HOLMES   Could you take me there?
RUBY   Maybe. Come along. *[Snuggles on to Holmes' arm]* Don't be shy of Ruby.

[They walk off as lights fade on street, coming up on the Den of Thieves. The Gang is sitting around talking, when Ruby and Holmes enter. Everyone looks up suspiciously]

BOB   'ere. Who's that?
RUBY   He's a new member of our gang – or at least he wants to be.
TOM   Don't be daft, we don't need no new members.
RUBY   Who says so? I like a healthy new member.
SAL   Another mouth to feed.
TOM   But we don't know nuffink about him. He could be anything, even a coppers' nark.
RUBY   He only just off a ship.
BOB   What ship you did just come off of?
HOLMES   If you really want to know, the *Marie Celeste*.
SAL   That sounds all right to me.
TOM   Think you're clever, eh?
HOLMES   Cleverer than any of you lot. I don't know what job you're working on, but whoever's in charge has surrounded himself with a right bunch of buffoons.
TOM   Who do you think you're calling buffoons?
HOLMES   I know who I'm calling names – I'd also call you milk sops.

BOB   *I say, steady on!*
TOM   *Do you want a think ear?*
HOLMES *You're the second person to offer me one today, but I'd be glad to return the compliment.* [Squares up to Tom]
BOB   *All right, calm down! You've only just arrived and already you're picking a fight.*
HOLMES *I just wanted to see how tough you lot was.*

[Enter Jim]

JIM   *Think you're tough, eh?*
HOLMES *Yeah. I've sailed the seven seas and seen many wonderful things and done some things so awful it'd make your toenails curl.*
TOM   *Yeah?*
HOLMES *Yeah.*

I'VE SAILED THE SEVEN SEAS

I've sailed the seven seas
  Through stormy waters,
I've led the mutineers
  And blood soaked slaughters.
I've slit from ear to ear
  A ship's commander,
then cast him in a boat
  For merest slander.

In each and every English county
Upon my head there is a bounty
For murder and again for rape;
Dame Fortune led me to escape!

GANG   *In each and every English county*
Upon his head there is a bounty
For murder and again for rape;
Dame Fortune led him to escape!

HOLMES *You ask me if I'm tough*
  I say 'yes' quickly,
But play it not too rough
  For I am prickly.
I've robbed a many bank
  For sportive pleasure
And only when I'd drank
  Thought on the treasure.

I've kidnapped men and asked for ransom
The proceeds of such acts are handsome,
Police attempts have failed to catch me.
I'll wager none of you can match me!

GANG   *He's kidnapped man and asked for ransom*
The proceeds of such acts are handsome,
Police attempts have failed to catch him.
He's right! We none of us can match him!

[This has been sung and acted in heroic style, with Holmes menacing various members of the gang in turn]

BOB   If just one of those stories is true you sound like the sort of man we need.

JIM   Who said we needed anyone else?

RUBY   Our Leader did say to me that he might need an extra hand.

SAL   But won't he look funny with three hands?

[The others all ignore her]

JIM   I don't like the idea of rushing into it like this. We hardly know anything about our friend here – we don't even know his name.

HOLMES   If it's of any interest to you, my name's John Clay.

JIM   John Clay. If that is your name, how come I've never heard of you?

HOLMES   Have you been to the West Indies?

JIM   No I haven't.

HOLMES   I do most of my work there.

BOB   Are you wanted by the police?

HOLMES   Of course.

TOM   There, we don't want someone who the police are after.

BOB   Why not? They're after you.

HOLMES   Anyway, they don't know I'm here and what they don't know won't hurt them.

RUBY   This isn't getting us anywhere. We should ask our Leader whether John can join us.

JIM   And if he doesn't?

TOM   Then we'll have to get rid of Mr John Clay. *[Makes throat slitting gesture]*

HOLMES   That doesn't scare me – I'm ready to meet your leader.

TOM   But that's the interesting thing, in this organisation you don't exactly meet the leader.

HOLMES   What do you mean?

BOB   You'll see. Ruby!

[Ruby pulls the curtain to reveal the speaker, as before.]

RUBY   Say 'hello' to our Leader.

HOLMES   What's this? Some kind of a joke? What is it? Is there a speaking tube or electrical wires or something?

BOB   That's not important. Just listen.

VOICE   Welcome, John Clay. I have listened to your conversation and know all about you. So you wish to join?

HOLMES   Yeah, as long as the money's good.

VOICE   The money will be very good if you do what I say. First, what do you know of our little enterprise?

HOLMES   Nothing.

VOICE   You have no doubt heard of the audacious kidnapping of Princess
Fatima at the Hyperian Music Hall in front of the British police?
HOLMES   No.
JIM   What? But it was all over the Town.
HOLMES   I was at sea, wasn't I?
VOICE   That job was carried out by us - a brilliant master plan that
will bring me in millions.
HOLMES   I'm impressed, but where do I fit in?
VOICE   I like your style and there's one or two little jobs that I think
you can do.
JIM   But doesn't he have to swear?
VOICE   That is not necessary. And do not question me again - you can
be replaced. I have not forgotten your behaviour at Lord Chumley's. Now, to
continue with our work.
RUBY   Yes, Leader.
VOICE   John, although I have accepted you, you will have to perform a
small duty to prove yourself worthy.
HOLMES   Anything you say.
VOICE   If you succeed, you will become a full member of my little
organisation - if you fail...
[Tom again draws his finger across his throat]

HOLMES   I understand: it don't scare me.
VOICE   For this part of the operation I require all of you to sign a
letter. What the letter is, is of no interest to you. I want each of you to
copy the signature on the piece of paper attached.
RUBY   Here they are, lads, come over here. Now just copy what's on
the bottom of this letter.

[Bob, Tom, Jim and Holmes queue up and sign one by one]
BOB   But if he has a copy, why don't he do it hisself?
HOLMES   Here, this is Sherlock Holmes's monniker.

[Ruby picks up the signatures and crumples one up in disgust]
RUBY   Which of you idiots signed with an 'X'? [Jim looks guilty]
VOICE   Which is closest?
RUBY   John Clay's.
VOICE   Very well. Put it in the box. [Ruby does so] Now for the little
job. Take that box to Mr Sherlock Holmes' rooms. I'm sure you know where
they are.
BOB   We certainly do.
VOICE   Make sure that box is found in his rooms. Do you think you can
manage that?
BOB   Yes.
TOM   Definitely.
JIM   A pleasure.
HOLMES   Of course.
SAL   What's the question?
BOB   Come along.

[Ruby gives the box to Bob. The gang, with Holmes, are about to exit
when Tom is called back]

VOICE   Tom! I will require you to wait a minute.
TOM   You don't mean I'm going to miss the action? You know how
impatient I've been.
VOICE   No, I've got a job which I think is more worthy of your
particular talents.
TOM   What do you mean?
VOICE   A chain is only as strong as its weakest link and there is a man
who is weakening by the minute.
TOM   You want me to remove that link?
VOICE   Yes, the man is Marvo the Magician. He is getting decidedly
jumpy. You will find him at the Hyperian Music Hall. Do a good job.
TOM   You can count on me.   [Exit]
RUBY   Here, I'm not sure that I want to be tied up with a murder.
VOICE   You won't be connected, but if you're getting nervous...
RUBY   No, it just came as a bit of a surprise.
VOICE   That's a good girl. [Ruby exits]
SAL   Where's everybody gone? [Exit]

[The lights fade on the Den of Thieves and come up on the Hyperian Music
Hall stage. The show is over and the cast is getting ready to go. Marvo
is on his own looking worried. Tilly goes over to him]

TILLY   Aren't you going home? You'd feel better in a nice warm bed.
BETH   Who with?
MARVO   I won't feel better 'til I'm out of all this.
TILLY   You can't get out of this, as you say.
BETH   Yeah, you're up to your neck in it like all of us. Why don't you
just make the best of it?
MARVO   Best of it, hah! I'm getting out. I could catch a boat to France
or maybe even America – if I could get my money now.
BARKER   This is no time for any of us to be getting windy. If we just sit
tight we'll be all right.
PEARL   That's right. When we get the money we'll be in clover. Then
you could travel round the world, if you want.
MARVO   What about the police? What if they get suspicious?
BARKER   They've already questioned you.
MARVO   What about Sherlock Holmes?
BETH   Sherlock Holmes is on the run and the police even suspect him
of the kidnapping – isn't it a scream?
MARVO   Then why aren't I laughing?
PEARL   Because you don't have the right outlook.
MARVO   Look, I'm frightened and I want to get out.
LILY   I know what you mean. We all feel nervous, but there's nothing
we can do. We're in this to our necks and we're going to have to put up
with it until the end.
ROSE   She's right, you know. Is this the great Marvo who performed
the seven sword trick, the wall of fire and the exploding tophat?
MARVO   But I was in control then – I'm not so sure now.
LILY   Don't worry!
MARVO   I don't know, maybe it would be better if I told the police all I
know and get it off my chest.

BARKER   *If a certain person hear you talking like that, you'd be for it.
When you get the money you'll feel better.*
MARVO   *Blood money.*
BARKER   *No one's been hurt yet. We just assisted in a little kidnapping,
so just be happy with what you've got and keep quiet or we could all be for
it.*
TILLY *That's right, just remember the words of the old music hall song.*
MARVO   *Music hall song? I'll give you a music hall song.*

SAUCE FOR THE GOOSE

*Sauce for the goose is sauce for the gander,
To this Boss I'll never more pander,
To Lestrade I'll speak with candour;
    Blood! Blood! There's blood on us all!*

CHORUS   *An eye for an eye and a tooth for a tooth,
That's what the Boss will say, forsooth,
If you to Lestrade reveal the truth;
    Bluff! Bluff! Your bluff we'll call!*

MARVO   *I fear this game no more can I play
    My hands now shake with fright,
I'll ne'er again my art betray,
    However poor my plight,
Men may come to take my life –
    I see it in the stars –
They'll use the ever-silent knife
    From which they all wear scars!*

*Sauce for the goose is sauce for the gander,
To this Boss I can never more pander,
To Lestrade I'll speak with candour;
    Blood! Blood! There's blood on us all!*

CHORUS   *We, my friend, are birds of a feather,
Bound, therefore, to stick together,
Upon your nerve keep tight the tether;
    Bluff! Bluff! Your bluff we'll call!*

LILY   *Well, I think it's time we all started for home. Think
about what we said, Marvo, it's for the best in the long run.*
MARVO   *I suppose you're right, but I can't help feeling bad.*
BETH   *Who cares about that, 'bye.*

[Enter Tom, menacingly]

TOM   *Good evening, ladies and gents.*
BARKER   *What do you think you're doing?*
TOM   *I've come 'ere to do a little job.   Which one of you two is
Marvo the Magician?*
MARVO *[stepping forward]*   *I'm Marvo. What do you want?*
TOM   *The Chief sent me to give you a message.*
MARVO   *Oh, yes? What is it?*
TOM   *He's found out that you're not altogether happy with our little*

enterprise and that you'd like to get out.
MARVO   So?
TOM   So – I've come to let you out, so to speak. *[Produces a knife]*
ROSE *[screams]* Oh, no.
LILY   You can't mean to...
BARKER   Look I've had a word with him and I'm sure he'll toe the line.
Now you don't want to cause any unpleasantness in this lovely theatre, do
you?
TOM   I come here to do a job and...
TILLY   Marvo! Run!

*[Marvo dodges behind the girls, who try to impede Tom's chase – but
keeping themselves out of the way of the knife. Marvo runs to a cabinet
upstage almost in the wings during the next two speeches]*

TOM   You don't get away that easy.
MARVO   You think not?
TOM   I've got you now, Marvo. You're a dead duck!

*[Marvo hurriedly gets into the cabinet and closes the door behind him.
There is a flash and an explosion and the cabinet falls open. Marvo has
vanished! (For construction of cabinet see Appendix)]*

TOM   Where'd he go?
LILY   Vanished into thin air.
TILLY   After all, he is a magician.
TOM   I know that, but there must be a trick to it. I mean he's got
to be somewhere.
BARKER   Like the young lady said – he's vanished. Now, I'm sure he
won't be any more trouble to you. Why don't you just go back and tell the
Boss that he's been disposed of?
TOM   I don't know what he's going to say about this. Anyhow, you lot
best not try anything or something might happen to you.
BARKER   Don't worry, we're loyal.
TOM   Maybe, but remember what I say. *[After menacing the group
individually with his knife, he puts it away, then exits]*
BETH   I can't stand people like that!
BARKER   I think we'd all better head home and keep quiet. Remember
what he said – if we don't toe the line we'll all be for it.
ROSE   He's right. Let's go home.

[The girls and Barker head towards one exit, Lily goes the other way]

TILLY   Hey, Lily, aren't you coming back to the digs?
LILY   Later, I've got to pay someone a little visit first.
BARKER   Just be careful. We want to see you again.

*[They all exit. The lights fade on the Hyperian Music Hall and come up
again on the outside of 221b Baker Street. Bob, Jim and Holmes approach
cautiously]*

BOB   Well, this is the place.
HOLMES   Are you sure?
BOB   Yes. Number 221b, Baker Street, everyone knows that's Sherlock
Holmes' place.

HOLMES   Oh, yes, of course.
JIM   The problem is, how do we get that box into his room without raising suspicions.
BOB   I know the answer and it's simple.
JIM   If you had it, it must be.
BOB   It's obvious. We simply take this box, take careful aim and chuck it through the winder.
JIM [stopping him] No!
HOLMES   If we stand around here much longer someone's going to come along and they might get suspicious.
BOB   He's right. Now we've all got to think. [They all ponder]
JIM   What if I shin up the drainpipe, force open the window and chuck it in?
BOB   Good idea - but there's no drainpipe near the window.
JIM   Maybe we could build one.

[Bob and Holmes just look at him]

BOB   That is the most ridiculous idea I've ever heard.
JIM   Maybe not.
BOB   What?
JIM   Well, if one of you bent over I could stand on his back.
BOB   You might have an idea there. I'll bend over and you jump on my back.
JIM   Rightio.

[Jim takes the box from Bob. Bob bends over, hands braced on knees, just as Jim is about to climb onto Bob's back, a Policeman enters. He looks at them suspiciously and Bob and Jim pretend they're searching for something on the ground]

POLICEMAN Hello, hello, hello. Lost something?
BOB   Er - we're looking for a copper.
POLICEMAN It looks like you've found one. [Laughs and exits]

[Bob and Jim get nervously to their feet and stare after the Policeman]

BOB   Boy, that was close. I thought you was meant to be keeping a look out, John.
HOLMES   I was, but he seemed to come out of nowhere.
BOB   Let's get on with it before he comes back.
JIM   It's no good. When you bent down I checked the height and I'd never be able to reach that window.
BOB   Well, what are we going to do? If we don't get that box into Holmes's rooms the Leader will have our guts for garters.
JIM   I think I've got it!
HOLMES   Well, don't give it to me.
JIM   No, if we make a sort of human pyramid, I should be able to reach the window. Then it'd be a simple job dropping it on his desk.
BOB   Good thinking. Let's give it a try before someone else comes along.

[Bob assumes a pose with hands cupped over a bent right knee]

JIM   Hey, John, aren't you going to join us?

HOLMES   No, I think I'd rather watch.

[Jim puts his left foot into Bob's cupped hands and gives a little jump. Bob lifts the cupped hands and Jim starts travelling upwards. Both, of course, crash to the ground]

HOLMES   Well, that didn't work, did it?
JIM   You got any better ideas?
HOLMES   As a matter of fact, I have. *[Picks box off ground and goes to the front door]*
BOB   What d'you think you're doing?
HOLMES   Shh. *[Knocks on door. Mrs Hudson opens it and pretends not to recognise Holmes]*
HUDSON   Well, what do you want? I'm very busy.
HOLMES   Sorry, lady. I was given this to deliver to Mr Sherlock Holmes. Will you make sure he gets it – it's very important. *[Hands her the box and leaves his hand out hopefully]*
HUDSON   Be off, you scallywag, you'll get no tip off me! *[Slams door]*
BOB   That was brilliant! You're really going to be an asset to us.
JIM   Yeah, that was great. I think we should celebrate with a quick drink at the Dog and Pullet.
HOLMES   Shouldn't we be getting back?
JIM   Yeah, I s'pose so. Let's go.

[As they exit, the lights fade down on Baker Street and up on the Den of Thieves, where Sal is stirring the pot, Ruby sitting at the table and Lily standing talking to the horn]

LILY   ... and I still don't like it, what you did at the theatre. It could have brought the police down on us.
VOICE   Tom knows what he's doing. He'd have tided up after.
LILY   And what about this Sherlock Holmes business? Isn't that playing with fire? I mean, kidnapping's one thing, but trying to frame Sherlock Holmes is another. He is the greatest detective in the world.
VOICE If it was anyone but you they'd be severely punished for questioning me like this. As to Mr Holmes, I know he is a great detective, in fact, I'm banking on it!
LILY   I don't understand.
VOICE   If I didn't know you better, I would say that you are allowing your heart to rule your head.
LILY   That's ridiculous.
VOICE   I can hear the gang returning. I suggest you leave, but stay close.
LILY   But why?
VOICE   That is the second time you have questioned me. I will not tolerate a third time.
LILY   Very well. *[Exit]*
VOICE   Close the curtains, Ruby. You know what to do.
RUBY   Yes.

[As she pulls the curtains over the horn, Bob, Tom, Jim and Holmes enter in high spirits]

RUBY   *Did you complete your missions?*
BOB   *I'll say we did.*
JIM   *In fact, it was John here who managed it.*
RUBY   *I always thought he'd be useful. And, Tom, we've heard of your doings in the theatre.*

THE OATH OF ALLEGIANCE

TOM   *Yes, I've set that scene.*
OTHERS   *And to Holmes' we've been.*
ALL   *We did not hurry*
Or show panic with a worry,
For we did impress
Since we all said 'yes'
To an oath of stern allegiance
And we'll never bear a grievance,
No we'll never bear a grievance
On an oath of stern allegiance,
And we'll never question orders
While the Boss repels the boarders,
For we always keep the oaths we swear!

RUBY   And now I have a message from our Leader. In recognition of your excellent work, he has decided that you should see your prize.
JIM *[to Holmes]* Wait 'til you see this!
HOLMES   I'm agog!
RUBY   My lords, ladies and gentlemen, I give you the one and only Princess Fatima, plus – wait for it – the Reverend Charles Samuels!
[Everyone cheers as Ruby pulls the curtain to reveal the Princess and Mr Samuels sitting back to back, with wrists tied behind them and gagged. Tom and Jim lift them down and stand them centre stage]

JIM *[bowing elaborately]* Your Princess-ship!
TOM   Your Grace, or whatever. I hope you find our humble abode to your liking. *[laughs]*
RUBY   That's enough. This, as you may have gathered, John, is our prize.
HOLMES   And we're going to get a big ransom for these?
RUBY   A Princess's ransom.
HOLMES   And what'll happen to them afterwards?
RUBY   That is not your concern. Our Leader has told me that there is one more job to complete before we can round this project off. You will all follow me.
BOB   But what about the Princess and the Reverend gentleman here?
RUBY   Old Sal can take care of them, can't you, Sal? I said can't you, Sal?
SAL   Pardon?
RUBY   I said you can take care of them.
SAL   Oh, yes, I can get hold of them, if you need them.
HOLMES   Well, let's get going. *[As he turns to go, Holmes deliberately trips over his own feet and falls to the ground]*

TOM   Clumsy!
RUBY   Are you all right?
HOLMES   Yes.*[Tries to stand, but his leg gives out]* Ow! I think I've twisted my ankle. I'll be all right.
RUBY   You'd best stay here. We won't be long and I think Sal could use the company.
SAL   No, I've got all I need.
BOB   You stay here. I think we can manage. Come on, lads.

[Ruby, Bob, Tom and Jim exit, leaving Holmes nursing his ankle. After a moment, he rises and hobbles over to sit by Sal]

HOLMES   Well, Sal, had a hard day?
SAL   I'll say; they work me from dawn 'til dusk. I've worked here for five months, man and beast, never any rest, never a thank you.
HOLMES   I sympathise. When I was tired when I was a little boy, my mother used to sing to me. Would you like to hear it?

[Sal nods. By the time the song has ended Sal has gone to sleep]

LULLABY

HOLMES

The sun now has wearied and rests 'til the morn,
Little one, close your eyes, wake with the dawn;
The Queen of the Night now will lighten your way
And guide you and keep you in safety 'til day.

The moon now is riding so high on the night,
Guarding and keeping you safe from all fright,
Tomorrow will dawn once again bright and clear
But now you must sleep, o my child, o my dear.

[Holmes touches Sal to make sure she is asleep and then walks over to the prisoners]

HOLMES   You're all right. *[Removes Princess's gag]*
FATIMA   You devil, I spit on you. *[Goes to do so]*
HOLMES   I'd rather you didn't. I have come to rescue you.
FATIMA   Who are you?
HOLMES *[untying the ropes on their wrists and removing the gag from Mr Samuels]* The name is Sherlock Holmes.
SAMUELS   Mr Holmes, the great detective? I've read Doctor Watson's marvellous stories about you.
HOLMES   Hasn't everyone?
FATIMA   But how did you know we were here?
HOLMES   I've been looking for you ever since you were abducted from the Hyperian.
FATIMA   But we never got to the music hall. I was kidnapped in the coach on the way there.
HOLMES   As I suspected. And I suppose you never visited me, Mr Samuels?
SAMUELS   No, I was adbucted with the Princess. I have never had the privilege of meeting you before, Mr Holmes.
HOLMES   I see, then we must move very quickly, as I know we're up

against an exceptionally dangerous adversary.
SAMUELS   I'll go and see if there's anyone about. *[Runs off]*
FATIMA   I don't understand.
HOLMES   I'll explain later, but first we must get out of here, they could
be back at any moment. Come along, Your Highness, if you would care to
step this way.
FATIMA   Where are you going to take me?

[Mr Samuels runs back into the room, carrying a walking stick]

SAMUELS   The coast is clear, but we must hurry.
HOLMES   I think not.
FATIMA   But you said we had to get away, they could be back at any
moment.
HOLMES   Ah, but you see, Princess, this is not the Reverend Charles
Samuels.
SAMUELS   That's ridiculous. You're not well, it must be the excitement.
FATIMA   What do you mean?
HOLMES   The man who ran from this room was the real Mr Samuels, but
this is none other than – *[he rips 'Mr Samuel's' beard off him]* – Colonel
James Moriarty, brother of the arch criminal, Professor Moriarty!
FATIMA   What!
MORIARTY Mr Holmes, I congratulate you. *[Calls]* Come in, all of you.
*[Enter Ruby, Bob, Tom and Jim, who take up positions round Holmes and
the Princess]*
HOLMES   You see, this is the man who visited me pretending to be your
guardian.
FATIMA   You devil! *[Goes to attack Moriarty, but is caught by Tom]*
Take your hands off me, you swine!
MORIARTY She has spirit, I must say that. Now, tell me, Mr Holmes, when
did you realise it was me?
HOLMES   I had my suspicions that you weren't genuine when you first
visited me. I detected a slight trace of the smell of bay rum. It would be
very unusual for a bearded gentleman to use such a substance, but I didn't
suspect it was you until much later when I found out how devious the plan
was. But, tell me, why are you trying to implicate me in this crime?
MORIARTY You killed my brother at the Reichenbach Falls. And I swore
then that I would get my revenge upon Sherlock Holmes.
HOLMES   So you came to London, kidnapped a Princess and a clergyman,
all for revenge on me?
MORIARTY I use who I like.
HOLMES   You obviously have such a fine brain, why couldn't you use it
for good. Think of the disgrace already on your family.
MORIARTY Ha! I do what I do best – like this little trap.
HOLMES   What do you mean?
MORIARTY You think I kidnapped the Princess for the ransom? No, it was
you I wanted, the man who sent my brother to his doom. That is why I
planted the deerstalker – to make sure you would be interested. I knew you
could not resist such a tempting and seemingly impossible case. The Princess

was a bait, you walked into the trap and then you know what I did.
SAL   Shut your trap.
MORIARTY Yes.

[Enter Lily Nightingale]

MORIARTY By the way, Mr Holmes, I'd like you to meet Miss Lily Nightingale. But, of course, you have already met.
LILY   I'm sorry.
HOLMES   How did you make her work for you?
MORIARTY If she doesn't, her brother will hang. I find it entertaining that
a man with a dislike of womankind should be trapped by two of them. You
see, Mr Holmes, when I heard you had run away from the police I guessed
that you would try to infiltrate my humble organisation, so despite your
disguise we knew it was you all along. Amusing, isn't it?
HOLMES   As amusing as that snake you left in my rooms.
MORIARTY Lily was very helpful with that; I thought it would get you
interested.
HOLMES   And the egg?
MORIARTY Egg?
HOLMES   Zactly. What are you going to do with us?
FATIMA   What have you done with my guardian, son of a pig?
MORIARTY Spirit can become a little tiresome. Take her away and keep
her quiet.
FATIMA   You devil!

[Tom drags her from the room. Lily slips away as well]

MORIARTY And now I would like to hear if you have worked out, with that
brilliant mind of yours, how the disappearance was managed.
HOLMES   It was an elementary trick. The idea was to make it seem as if
Princess Fatima disappeared from the Hyperian stage. To that end you
kidnapped Mr Samuels and the Princess from their carriage on the way to
the theatre. You had to get her bodyguard out of the way, so you gave him
a mild laxative.
SAL   Not that mild.
HOLMES   Then you and, I believe, Ruby here, cleverly made up to like
like the Princess, took their places. The music hall performers were all in on
it, so when Marvo asked for a volunteer Ruby, as the Princess, immediately
stood up. Once on stage, as she is of petite stature, she was given a box to
stand upon, then she was covered in a sheet and the fake jewels placed upon
the dummy.
MORIARTY Pray continue.
HOLMES   Now came the clever part. Ruby is a skilled contortionist and,
when the jewels burst into flame, distracting the audience's attention, she
folded herself into the small box and disappeared. In the ensuing commotion
it was easy for the box to be dragged off stage, when Ruby extrictade herself and removed her make-up. It was by chance that Doctor Watson
discovered the box and that I noticed a trace of grease paint on the lid. You
had used the magician's traditional ploy of misdirection.
MORIARTY Congratulations, Mr Holmes. What a pity it is that it will be
your last deduction.

RUBY   *We should never have let him take that box.*
MORIARTY *Yes. Now, Mr Holmes, I suppose you think you're clever?*
HOLMES   *I don't think, I know. But you should meet my brother Mycroft.*
MORIARTY *I tire of you, Mr Holmes, but you will not bother me again. [He pokes the ferrule of his walking stick into Holmes' leg] It has been a pleasure knowing you.*
HOLMES   *You fiend, what have you done?*
MORIARTY *It's a mild poison; don't worry, it won't kill you.*
HOLMES   *You inhuman monster... [He sways and buckles at the knees, Bob and Jim hold him up]*
MORIARTY *Come! [Exeunt omnes]*

[The curtains close and Moriarty steps in front of them. While he is singing his song a tressel table with Holmes on it is brought on to the 'Hyperian stage' and the curtains rise towards the end of the song so that Moriarty can gloat over Holmes]

MORIARTY!

MORIARTY   He killed a man at the Reichenbach Falls,
                                A man who was my brother;
                     And sweet revenge now therefore calls,
                                I owe it to our mother.
                     Moriarty! Moriarty! Moriarty's the name,
                     Holmes is outnumbered and now he's the game.

                     His end I've planned with utmost care
                                And method quite ingenious;
                     He's walked into my little snare
                                Which I had set so devious.
                     Moriarty! Moriarty! Moriarty am I,
                     Holmes is outwitted and surely must die.

                     At mercy of my hand you lay
                                As yet in peaceful slumber;
                     From execution there's no stay
                                You'll no more me encumber.
                     Moriarty! Moriarty! His brother I remain,
                     Soon Holmes to death elementary and plain.
                     Moriarty! Moriarty! His brother I remain,
                     Soon Holmes to death, so you'll struggle in vain.

MORIARTY *Wake up. [Slaps Holmes' face] Wake up. You're not dead – yet.*
HOLMES *[recovering consciousness] Where am I?*
MORIARTY *You are in the Hyperian Music Hall where it all began and where, for you, it will end.*
HOLMES   *You... I can't move.*
MORIARTY *No, I injected you with a unique drug which will paralyse your body, so that you can't move, except for your mouth.*

43

HOLMES   What are you going to do with me?
MORIARTY Now, that's the clever part. As you can see, there is a large sand bag, which is used as a counterweight, hanging above your head. Now, when this timing device - [Ruby brings on a metronome-type device and starts it ticking] - reaches zero, it will released this cord and the bag will fall smashing your head to pulp.
HOLMES   But why go to such bother, why not sheet me and have done with it?
MORIARTY That wouldn't suit my plan at all. You destroyed my brother, now I'm more than killing you, I'm destroying your reputation. It will be put around that the kidnap was your plan and that when it went disastrously wrong, you killed yourself with a characteristically ingenious mode of suicide.
HOLMES   No one will ever believe you.
MORIARTY Mud sticks, especially when it's backed up with the facts of your running from the police and the confession note which you so kindly signed and delivered.
HOLMES   You'll never get away with this.
MORIARTY But it looks as if I am. You now have about three minutes and, just to add to the excitement, the effects of the drug will wear off in about three and a half minutes. It will be comical to think of you praying that my timing is out. Ruby, I want you to stay with the other members of the music hall.
RUBY   I want to come with you. I want to make sure I get my money.
MORIARTY Don't worry. You'll all get what's coming to you.
RUBY   That's not fair. [Exit]
HOLMES   You're insane.
MORIARTY You are lying beneath a counterweight and calling me insane?
BOB [entering] The boat's ready.
MORIARTY Excuse me, Mr Holmes, I've got an appointment with a watery Saint. You once called my brother the Napoleon of crime.
HOLMES   May I remind you that Napoleon met his Waterloo.
MORIARTY But Napoleon's brother continued to reign as King. Au revoir, Mr Holmes - or should I say, good-bye.   [Laughs]

[Exit Moriarty and Bob, leaving Holmes on the table with the device ticking away. He struggles as best he can, but to no avail. Suddenly Dr Watson rushes in a peers around. At first he doesn't notice the table mid-stage]
WATSON   I say, Holmes?
HOLMES   Watson, over here, quickly.'
WATSON   [gazes round, focuses on Holmes and runs over to him]What has happened to you? Why are you lying down there?
HOLMES   No time to explain. Stop the timer or the counterweight will fall.
WATSON   What timer? Oh, I say. [He struggles with the timer, with no success. The ticking gets louder] I can't, the darned thing won't stop.

[He goes back to the timer, but still can't stop it. As it goes 'ping', Watson drags Holmes off the table. The second he is clear the counter-weight falls. Watson and Holmes are in a heap on the floor]

HOLMES   Thank you, Watson, you saved my life.
WATSON   Think nothing of it.
HOLMES   I can't explain it all now, but Moriarty's behind the kidnapping.
WATSON   Moriarty? But I though he was dead.
HOLMES *[rubbing his arms and legs as feeling returns]* So he is, this is Colonel James Moriarty, the Professor's brother. He seems to be out on his timing, feeling is coming back to me. By the way, Watson, how on earth did you find me?
WATSON   Well, I found that note you slipped into that box you gave to Mrs Hudson with the address of the Den of Thieves. When I got there I only found an old lady, but luckily for you I managed to find out from her where they'd taken you.
HOLMES   How did you do that? She's hard of hearing.
WATSON   A sovereign seemed to help her hearing.
HOLMES   Well, done, old chap. Now, they mentioned a boat and a watery Saint. That must mean that they're trying to escape in a boat from St Katherine's Dock. I've got to go and stop them. I hope it's not too late for the Princess.
WATSON   I'll come with you, I feel like a fight.
HOLMES   No. You find a telephone and tell Inspector Lestrade to meet me at St Katherine's. I'll need all the help I can get.
WATSON   Right.
[Exit Holmes, walking a little stiffly]
WATSON   I say, where is the telephone? Oh dear me! *[Ambles off]*
[The lights fade to blackout, under cover of which the table and timing device are struck. A couple of barrels are introduced and gentle water noises are heard, as the lights come up to St Katherine's Dock]
[Enter Moriarty, Ruby, Bob, Tom and Jim]
MORIARTY Gentlemen, everything seems to be proceeding according to plan. The police will be discovering Holmes' body in about an hour, by which time we will be long gone.
BOB   The Princess and the Reverend are safely on board the ship. What do you want done with them?
MORIARTY When we get clear away we will get the ransom – and then their bodies will be found floating in the Thames. Where's Lily?
RUBY   She was here a minute ago.
MORIARTY We can't wait for her. Come on.

[As Moriarty goes to lead the others off, Holmes enters behind them]
HOLMES   Not so fast, Colonel Moriarty.
MORIARTY Mr Holmes, I really must congratulate you on your powers of escape, but you're too late. As you see you are outnumbered.
TOM   Let me get at him.
HOLMES   As I thought, you have to hide behind thugs.
MORIARTY So you want a man to man fight, Marquis of Queensbury rules. I'm always ready to oblige. You lot, get on the barge, I will join you in a moment.

[Ruby, Bob and Jim exit, pulling Tom off with them]

HOLMES   So, at last. Face to face. And this time will be the last time,
Moriarty.
MORIARTY Did you think I would brawl like a common ruffian? You beat
my brother, but this time I have the advantage!

[He produces a gun and is about to fire when there is a small commotion
off stage distracting him. Holmes seizes the opportunity and dives for
Moriarty. A brief struggle ensues, then Inspector Lestrade and a policeman enter]

LESTRADE   That'll be enough of that, Moriarty, we've captured your men;
now we've got you!

[Moriarty pushes Holmes into Lestrade's path and jumps on to a barrel]

HOLMES   Look out! He's got a gun!
MORIARTY Stand back!
LESTRADE   Put that gun down, laddie, you'll only make it worse for your-
self. We've got this place surrounded.
MORIARTY Ha! He who fights and runs away, lives to fight another day, eh,
Sherlock?   [He leaps into the wings from the barrel (into the Thames).
There is a splash. Holmes, Lestrade and the policeman rush to the 'dock
edge'. There is a moment's silence]
POLICEMAN Not a sign of him.
LESTRADE   He must be a gonner.
HOLMES   You may be right, but I'm not so sure. I'm not so sure.
POLICEMAN I'll go and check the prisoners, sir. [Exit]
LESTRADE   Well, another case satisfactorily completed.
HOLMES   Yes, but I only wish we could be sure about Moriarty. I don't
think we've heard the last of him.
WATSON [entering, puffed] Holmes, my old friend, are you all right?
HOLMES   Yes, thank you, Watson, but I wouldn't be if it wasn't for your
telephone call to the police.
WATSON   But that's just the thing, I couldn't find a confounded telephone
anywhere.
HOLMES   Then who rang Lestrade?
LESTRADE   It wasn't Doctor Watson. No, it was a woman who gave us the
tip-off.
WATSON   A woman? I wonder who that could have been?

[A heavily muffled figure walks across the stage a says in a husky
voice...]

LILY   Well done, Sherlock. [Exit]
LESTRADE   Here, who was that?
HOLMES   Just a friend, a very dear friend.
POLICEMAN [entering] Excuse me, sir. The Princess says she wants a word
with Mr Holmes.

[Enter Princess Fatima, with a blanket wrapped round her shoulders]

HOLMES   Good evening, Your Highness. I hope you are well.
FATIMA   Oh yes, I am well, thanks to you. And my guardian is recovering
from the bang on the head he received. I just had to see you to tell you
how grateful I am for saving me.

HOLMES   Thank you, Princess, but I couldn't have done it without Doctor Watson here.
FATIMA   Oh, Doctor Watson, who writes all those wonderful stories?
HOLMES   And, of course, our constabulary.
LESTRADE   Our pleasure, ma'am.
FATIMA   All I can say is that I'm grateful to you all, as shall be my entire country. Here is a ring, Mr Holmes, for you to remember me by.
HOLMES *[accepting ring from Fatima's finger]* I am most honoured, Your Highness.
WATSON   I say, that's worth a Princess's ransom!
POLICEMAN Well, Miss, we'd better be getting you somewhere warm.
FATIMA   Yes, but, once again, I must thank you all for my life and for getting rid of those awful people. *[Exit Fatima and Policeman]*
LESTRADE   Well, you've done it again, Mr Holmes.
HOLMES   Just doing what I do best.
LESTRADE   Oh, no, it's more than that. We may have had our differences in the past, but I've said it before and I'll say it again: Mr Holmes, you are indeed the greatest detective in the world!

I CANNOT FIND THE WORD

LESTRADE

> I cannot find the word
> > Except in cliche hollow
> For seeing as not absurd
> > The clues I chanced to follow.
>
> Again to Holmes my thanks
> > To you, the injured party,
> My erroneous judgement ranks
> > With crimes of Moriarty.

HOLMES

> Though fled upon a barge
> > I vow to rich and poor,
> Some day he'll face his charge
> > And bear the full force of the law!

WATSON

> Now give three cheers for the man who fears
> For everyone's safety except his own;
> Although at first it appeared the worst
> We all of us must our thoughts atone!

[During this song, the entire cast has quietly assembled on stage in their final line-up formation]

WATSON   Hip, hip!
ALL   Hurrah!   *[repeated three times, of course]*

ELEMENTARY MY DEAR WATSON

CHORUS
>
> Elementary, my dear Watson,
> He seems frequently to say,
> His powers of deduction
> Make things clear as any day.
> The shred of cotton on a coat
> Or lying on the floor,
> May prove of no importance
> Or could open up a door;
> At every scrap of evidence
> You must know how to look,
> Until it's so familiar
> That you read it like a book,
> He cannot tell us how it's done
> For now we're near the end

WATSON
> I suppose it was quite elementary?

HOLMES
> Yes, dear friend!

CHORUS
>
> Now Watson here has chronicled
> The cases all to date,
> It's evident he's taken pains
> To get the record straight.
> We hope your publication fees
> Still handsomely compare,
> Without his little mysteries
> You'd have no income there.
> The welcome reappearance
> Of a beautiful Princess,
> He found the culprit very soon
> With typical success,
> He cannot tell us how it's done
> For now we're near the end.

WATSON
> I suppose again it's elementary?

HOLMES
> Yes, dear friend!

ACT ONE

On stage: In Holmes' rooms:
            2 chairs, with antimacassars
            Small table. On it: Stick telephone, newspapers, scissors, scrap book
            Rug
            On Mantlepiece: Test tubes in rack, pipe, 'relics'
            In Hearth: Fender, fire irons including poker
        In Thieves' Den:
            Table : On it: 2 bottles beer, 3 mugs
            2 seats
            Cooking pot with ladle
            At rear of set, over 3 ft flat, Curtains
            Behind curtains: [on table] Gramophone horn, with microphone attachment
        On Hyperian Music Hall stage:
            Box (which should appear to be in Thieves' Den set)
Off stage:
            Pouch of tobacco (WATSON)
            Sovereign (HOLMES)
            Starting pistol [with bang] (RUBY)
            Wicker basket (LILY)
            Bowl of eggs [with 1 hardboiled, 1 fresh] (JOE)
            Half-sovereign (HOLMES)
            Snake (WATSON)
            Police whistle (LESTRADE)

ACT TWO

On stage: In Thieves' Den:
            On Table: 4 letters, pen, ink pot, cigar box
Off stage:
            Basket (MRS HUDSON)
            Flick knife (TOM)
            Cord and gags for FATIMA and SAMUELS
            Walking stick (MORIARTY)
            Tressel table, 'timer', counterweight in flies
            Gun (MORIARTY)
            Blanket (FATIMA)
            Ring (FATIMA)

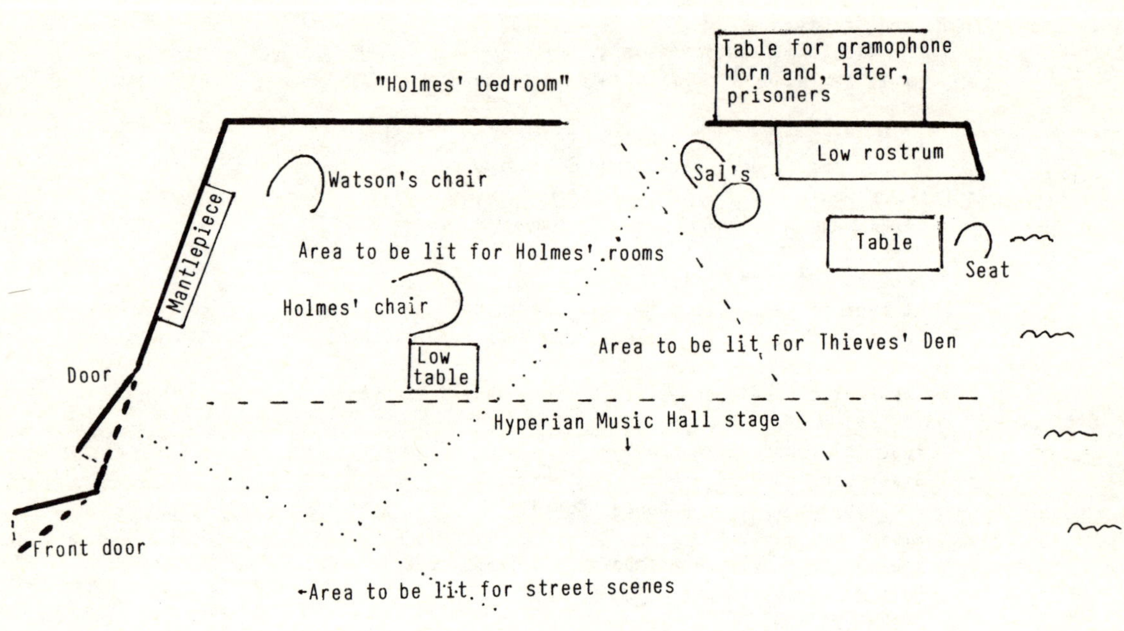

MARVO'S DISAPPEARING DOOR

A cube, approximately 3' x 3' x 6' is constructed of chipboard. The two sides are solid and joisted top and bottom. The back is hinged to the top joist, while the door is hinged to the up-stage side. All is painted black inside and out.

When Marvo is inside the cube a flash should be set off, to conceal his exit through the flapped back both from Tom and the audience.

The cube must, of course, be positioned adjacent to the wings.